Anonymous

Record of the Proceedings of the Sabbath School Teachers' Convention

SALZWASSER
VERLAG

Anonymous

Record of the Proceedings of the Sabbath School Teachers' Convention

Reprint of the original, first published in 1857.

1st Edition 2023 | ISBN: 978-3-37515-478-3

Verlag (Publisher): Salzwasser Verlag GmbH, Zeilweg 44, 60439 Frankfurt, Deutschland
Vertretungsberechtigt (Authorized to represent): E. Roepke, Zeilweg 44, 60439 Frankfurt, Deutschland
Druck (Print): Books on Demand GmbH, In de Tarpen 42, 22848 Norderstedt, Deutschland

DESIGNATION OF SCHOOL. LOCALITIES. (rs in the left hand column refer to pages, &c.)	1. How many teachers are there in your school?	2. What is the average attendance of teachers?	3. How many scholars are there in your school?	4. What is the average attendance of scholars?	5. How many of the scholars are over 15 years of age?	6. How many are under six?	7. Compared with previous years, is your school prosperous; and if so, what was the increase during the past year, —or otherwise what was the loss?	Gain.	Loss.	8. Is your school closed during any portion of the year?	9. Is it suffering from any particular cause?	10.
abyterian Church of Canada,	14	11	76	54	1	10	Prosperous.	10		Open all the year...	No...	Non
. E. Church,	18	10	76	41		20	Prosperous.			No...	No...	Ten
... ...	8	7	60		1		Decrease. Another school opened...		15	No...	No...	Non
... ...	8	8	80	50	10		Increase.			No...	For want of a superintendent.	...
ist,	12	10	50	40	2	16	Prosperous.	10		No...	No...	Non
renix Union,	10	8	40	25		6	None to notice...			During winter.	For want of ministerial labor.	...
rican Presbyterian, branch School.	12	12	93	60	20	10	Stationary.			No...	No...	Thr
... ...	8	7	73	42	24		Increase.	10		Winter.	No...	No.
... ...	6	6	35	20			Stationary.	30		During 4 months...	From negligence of parents...	Non
eyan Methodist District School.	12	10	90	60	2		Prosperous, very.	45		No...	Want of efficient teachers.	One.
terian Church of Canada,	8	6	60	50	25	7	Same as last year.			No...	Intemperance of some parents.	Non
lission,	12	8	140	95	17	22	Several have left.			No...	No...	Six.
Union,	12	10	80	60	18		About same.			No...	No...	Non
k st. Presb. Church of Canada,	17	17	117	80	0	15	Prosperous.	10		During winter.	No...	Non
... ...	7	4	35		4		Increase.	44		No...	No...	Twe
... ...	23	21	176	110	20		Prosperous.	40		No...	No...	Fou
eyan,	18	14	170	130	2		Yes.	40		No...	Indifference in parents. Irregularity in teachers.	Twe
yan,	12	8	125	80	22		Moderately prosperous.	40		No...	From want of accommodation.	Thr
byterian Church of Canada,	8	5	40	45	12		Prosperous.	27		No...	No...	One.
t, Durham,	9	9	60	43	14		Fewer on books. Attendance more regular.			During winter.	For want of system, and irregularity of teachers.	Non
urch,	4	7	50	30	3		Prosperous.			No...	Parents not interested.	Non
... ...	7	7	50	50	0		Improving.			No...	Want of proper books...	Non
odist, New Connexion,	13	9	97	60	10		Not very prosperous.	6		No...	Increase of other schools.	Non
... ...	11	8	82	47			Very prosperous.			No...	No...	Non
an,	15	10	90	70	5		Prosperous.			No...	No...	
... ...	8	6	40	24	6		Seems to be prosperous.	26		No...	Church burned ; just opened again.	
on,	11	11	100	60	10		Increase.	20		No...	No...	Non
od Presbyterian,	8	7	65	50	6		Yes.	2		No...	No...	Twe
tive Methodist,	43	37	263	124	31		Very prosperous.	100		No...	No...	Twe
rn Union,	6	5	50	30	6		Some increase.			Want of interest.		
... ...	8	8	40	20								Non
... ...	10	9	70	50	4		Prosperous.	25		No...	No...	Non
... ...	2	2	14	14			Increase.	4		No...	Want of teachers.	Twe
leyan,	10	7	60	35	5		Increase.	23		No...	Lack of zeal.	Thr
... ...	7	6	37	20	6		Prosperous.	12		No...	None.	Non
resbyterian Church of Canada,	7	6	60	50	12		...			Place of meeting not central.		Non
an,	6	5	35	20	4		Increase.			In winter sometimes.	Want of library, &c. ...	Eigh
Union,	30	20	207	120	36		Prosperous.	27		No...	No...	...
. E., Wesleyan,	5	8	50	50	16		About same.			No...	Non-attention of parents.	One.
. E., Baptist,	6	5	50	40	6		Prosperous.	10		No...	Not that we know of.	Non
Union,	6	5	40	29	6		Prosperous.			During winter.	Not that we know of.	Nov
... ...	4	2	20	15	10		Prosperous.			No...	Yes...	One.
. E., Congregational,	7	5	37	22	12		Visible improvement.			No...	No...	One.
... ...	18	16	80	60	2		Average about same.			During winter.	No...	Non
... ...	5	4	38	30	11		Only open one year.			No...	For want of teachers...	Five
... ...	2	1	14	8	10		Only in first year.			No...	We think so.	me.
re, Lampton, "Providence," Bible Christian,	10	8	39	32			Only four months started.	12		No...	Rather cramped for time.	Thir
... ...	24	21	108	70	9		Increase.	15		No...	No...	Ten.
an,	14	10	70	55			Increase.			No...	None.	Two
... ...	13	13	75	63	9		Progress satisfactory.			No...	No...	One.
... ...	3	3	40	38	4		About same.			No...	No...	Thir
... ...	14	13	90	64	12		Prosperous.			No...	Not sensibly.	l mo.
eyan,	20	15	65	60	24		Prosperous.	30		No...	Want of spirituality and new library.	Non
on,	9	8	87	60	11		Prosperous.			No...	Yes...	Non
... ...	4	4	40	30	4		Prosperous.			No...	No...	Non
rch of England,	2	2	38	38	5		Prosperous.			No...	No...	Thr
... ...	2	2	22	18			Only commenced this year.			No...	No...	Non
... ...	7	6	36	20			Commenced November, 1856.			No...	Want of a library.	Two
national,	23	16	75	60	30		About stationary.			No...	No...	Eigh
wrence Suburbs Wesleyan,	8	8	135	60	13		Prosperous.			During winter.	No...	Non
ptist	10	8	40		40		Not much change.	12		No...	No...	Fou
nitive Methodist,	6	4	60	25	4		Increasing.			No...	No...	Non
t,	11	10	60	60	7		Opened last summer...		10	No...	No...	Fou
nezor,	10	4	33	20			Decided advance in scholars...			No...	No...	Non
erian,	11	10	73	63	35		Yes. Without increase.	3		No...	Want of teachers.	Non
Wesleyan,	12	10	80	65	9		Increase.	15		No...	No...	Six.
Wesleyan,	17	13	90	60			Stationary.			No...	No...	Non
Presbyterian Church of Canada,	12	10	70	60	5		Prosperous.	20		No...	Want of teachers.	Non
American Presbyterian,	11	11	68	61	5		Prosperous.	24		No...	Without a pastor.	Non
Baptist,	18	16	208	118	10		Not so prosperous.		10	No...	Removal of some teachers.	Two
... ...	9	7	80	50	6		Prosperous.	40		Yes.	None.	Thr
Street Baptist,	34	30	234	180	22		Prosperous.	60		No...	From a want of appreciation.	Non
th Monaghan,	7	6	70	54	12		Very prosperous.			No...	Want of books.	Two
an,	3	3	40	33	4		Increasing.	5		During winter.	Our building is small.	Two
hapel Union,	3	3	24	20			Increase.			No...	None.	Non
iate Presbyterian Church,	...	...	...	...			About the same.			No...	No...	Two
ian Church of Canada,	17	15	12	100	6		Very prosperous.	14		No...	Not sufficiently appreciated...	Ton
, Warwick,	8	8	31	32	6		Rather on the increase.			No...	No...	Fou
k Presbyterian Church of Canada.	8	8	67	40			Prospers greatly.			No...	No...	Thr
Christian,	7	6	45				Prosperous.			No...	None.	Non
... ...	28	12	106	98	6		Only fourteen months opened.	20		No...	Irregularity of teachers.	Fou
ners Presb'n Church of Canada,	17	15	117	84	1		Prosperous.	10		No...	Temporary decrease, from sickness.	Four
l Presbyterian,	9	8	33	32			A little progress...	14		No...	No...	Non
tive Methodist,	11	16	7	55			Increase.	10		No...	Want of teachers.	One
, Sayer Street,	14	12	88	45								

RETURNS.

How many ... the scho-... are ... members of church?	11. How many would not be under any religious instruction, were it not for the Sabbath School?	12. How many books does your library contain?	13. Have you a regular Teachers' Meeting; and if so, is it for prayer, or for the study of lesson, or both?	14. What is the average attendance at Teachers' Meeting?	15. How many, if any, were the conversions in your school during the past year?	16. Is your school in the habit of doing anything for Missions?	17. Are the people in y... alive to the importan... Sabbath Schoo...
	Think a great part of them...	120	First Monday each month (both).	11	Cannot say if any.	A little to P. C. Mission.	Generally.
	Not any.	250	No regular, only for business occasionally.	9	Fifteen.	Not anything.	Generally.
	Several.	200	No regular meeting.			Nothing.	Not very.
	Cannot tell.	300	No meeting; teachers live too far off.	7	Cannot say.	Yes.	Rather backward.
	Hard to say; certainly some.	180	Weekly, for both.			Yes.	Believe so.
		30	No.		Hope a few.	Annually for Tract Society.	Lukewarm.
	A small number—say six.	200	No; teachers too much scattered.	8	None.	They are.	A good deal.
	Not known.	300	No.		None.	No.	They are.
	Few, if any.	100	Once a quarter, for prayer.	6	None known.	Yes, £40 last year.	Not at all.
	About forty.	100			None known.	Yes, for African Mission.	Yes.
	The majority.	175	Once a quarter, to transact business.		Not known.		Generally no.
	About twenty.	820	Yes, for prayer and consultation.	17		Yes, a Missionary Box.	To some extent.
		300	Only occasionally teachers as scattered.	21	One.	Yes.	Generally.
	Nearly all receive instruction at home.	310	Yes, for prayer.	20	Cannot say.	Some children are collectors.	Not generally.
	Not many—cannot say.	200	Twice in the season; prayer, &c.			Yes, £60 this year.	Not as should.
	About fifty.	550	Prayer monthly, lessons weekly.			Yes, £00 Wesleyan Mission.	Much indifference.
	Cannot state positively.	210	Semi-quarterly, for business.	8		It is not.	Some are.
	All connected with church.	300	None at present.			Juvenile Missionary Society.	Yes.
	One-fourth.	270	Revision of lessons.		None known.	Occasionally.	No.
	Very few.	300	Every Sabbath, study of lesson.		None known.	Yes.	Yes.
		100	None, but feel need of one.				Small portion.
	Eight.	200	Weekly, for prayer.				Increasing.
	Say twenty-five.	100	No, only business meetings.	6	Not aware of any.	Three teachers, active collectors.	Partially.
	Twelve.	300	No, but intend to have one.		One.	Yes.	Partial.
	About thirty-five.	250	None, about to establish one.	8			Beginning to be...
	Forty-five.	300	No regular, but when held, prayer.		I fear none.	Not yet.	Some are.
		170	Both.			Yes.	Generally.
	Many have no other means.	048	Prayer.	19	Twelve.	Not last year.	Not all.
		187	Business meeting once a month.	5	Numb. under serious impressions.	No.	Not all.
	Fifty.	175	For both.			No.	Improving.
		20	For prayer and lesson, weekly.		Two under serious impressions.	No.	They are not.
	Seventeen.	200	No.			No.	No.
	None.	100	Yes, to devise plans for success.		Eight.	No.	Generally.
		200	No.		None.	Not yet.	Very much.
	Cannot say.	75	One, for prayer only.			No.	Some.
	None.	200	Not regular, teachers too scattered.		Cannot say.	Yes.	Growing.
	Twenty.	150	Prayer and business once each month.	15	Can't say.	For Missionary and Bible Society.	Too much apathy.
	Not more than four.	800	None.		One.	No.	Generally.
	A number, but cannot say how many.	400	None.		None.	To China Testament Fund.	Partial.
	Seventeen.	125	None.		Year none.	About to commence.	No.
	None.	150			None.	No.	No.
	Nine.	200	Yes.		None.		Portion are.
	Fifteen.	200	None yet.			Juvenile Missionary Society.	Partial.
	One.	400	None.		One.	No.	Only a few.
	None.	110	None.			None.	Very little.
			None.			Do a little.	We trust so.
two	Very few.	50	Yes.			None.	Partial.
	Thirteen.	150	Regular, for prayer and improvement.	8	None.	No.	Yes.
	None.	100	Not regular, for business chiefly.	11	Thirty-four.	No.	Not sufficiently so.
		400			Seven.	No.	Not general.
B.	Eight.	161	For both, once a month.	8	None.	Collection on Sabbath.	Not very much.
	Thirty.	250	We have, for study of lesson.	10	Fifteen.	Occasionally.	Generally.
	None.	100	We have occasional, for both.	9	Three.	No.	Some are, some not.
	All far from any place of worship.	400	One for prayer just organized.		None.	Yes.	Partially so.
	All of them.	300			None.	No.	Apparently.
	The majority.	70	No, about to commence one.			No.	Not as much as should.
	Six.	270				No.	Not very favorable.
	One-third.		No, concert for prayer monthly.	15	Ten.	For 1856, £25 3s. 6d.	Yes, generally.
four	None.	150	Monthly meeting, for prayer.		One.	No.	Moderately so.
	One-half.	300	No.			Yes.	I think they are.
	Six.	82	No.			Yes.	Increasingly so.
	A large number.	120	No.		Six.	Yes.	Yes.
	None.	300	No.	10	None.	A Missionary Box.	Generally yes.
	Can't say.	200	No.		None.	No.	Not fully alive.
	Some.	105	A monthly meeting, prayer and business.		None.	No.	Not fully alive.
	Twenty.	200			Don't know.	No.	No.
	Ten.	500	Yes, for both.	8	None.	No.	But partially.
	Twenty.	250	Monthly, prayer and conference.		Three.	Yes.	Not so much as desirable.
	Two.	150	Yes, both.	8	Two.	No.	Generally so.
	Eighty.	600	Once a month, prayer.	12	Twelve seriously inclined.	Yes.	No.
	One-half.	200	Irregular, study of lesson.	8	None.	For Bible Society, £19	Yes.
	Cannot tell.	600	Prayer and business.	14	Fifteen.	No.	They are.
	None.	100	No.		None.	Monthly collections.	Generally alive.
	One-fourth.	184			None.	None.	Yes.
		100				Yes.	Yes.
		150					Yes.
	Don't know.	250	Yes, for study of lesson.	8	Couldn't say.	Yes.	Most are.
	No other means within seven miles.	150	Yes, attended by whole settlement, 96 souls.		No.	No.	Very much so.
	Thirty.	125	No.			No.	Partially indifferent.
		170	No.		None known.	No.	To some extent.
	Not many.	123	No, only when business requires.	10	Four.	Yes.	Moderately.
	Don't know.	300	One weekly, for lessons, one for prayer.	10	None known.	Yes.	Perhaps not sufficient.
	Not any.	223	Weekly, both, also monthly prayer.	7	Believe good is done.	Yes.	Reason to think not.
			Monthly, for business.	6	One.	Yes.	Not generally.
	Think none.	120	Weekly, both.	7	Believe a few.	Yes, every Sabbath.	Not generally.

DESIGNATION OF SCHOOL. LOCALITIES. (numbers in the left hand column refer to of debates, &c.)	1. How many teachers are there in your school?	2. What is the average attendance of teachers?	3. How many scholars are there in your school?	4. What is the average attendance of scholars?	5. How many of the scholars are over 16 year, of age?	6. How many are under six?	7. Compared with previous years, is your school prosperous and if so, what was the increase during the past year, — or otherwise what was the loss?	8. Is your school closed during any portion of the year?		9. Is it suffering from any particular cause?	10. How m of th ... laws ... ... number the ...
								Gain.	Lost.		
...lle Wesleyan,	7	6	50	40	10	6	Much the same...	No...		Church will not take hold of the work as it should	Ten...
...alls,	10	8	51	41	12		5 Prosperous...	No...	1		Name...
...		14	113	80			4 Increase...	In winter...		Want of different books,	Four...
... Wesleyan,	6	5	55	3?	1?		10 Encouraging,	No...	2?		
...al Event Union,		5	61	61	2?		About the same,	No...		No...	Three...
...le, Campbell's Cross,	17	18	15?	102	1?		5 Yes...	No...		No...	None...
...rn,		6	45				13 Increase,	No...	5	Want of interest.	
...	5	4	84	4?	7		2 Decrease...	No...			
...CC. U.	4	4	84	20	6		4 dart to say,	No...	2?	Want of teachers,	None...
...o Congregational Church,	12	10	90	40			14 Increase,	No...	2?	Want of proper interest,	Three...
...nion,	17	17	13?	70	10		15 Increased,	No...		Want of teachers,	One...
...e Baptist,	4	4	2?	1?			4 Stationary,	No...		Want of attention,	None...
...Congregational,	7	4	3?	2?	8		19 Prosperous.	No...	1?	Want of energy,	One-th...
...n York, Slayter's Corners,		6	40				16 only eleven months open.	No...		Want of more pious teachers,	None...
...ston,	10	6	57	4?			12 About six months open. Prosperous.	No...		Want of library going to get one...	None...
...ern,		5	77	5?	1?		4 Stationary,	No...		for want of more interest,	Five...
...Christian,		8	117	5?	1?		5 Yes,	No...		Want of encouragement.	Fifteen...
...		4	2?	1?	2		2 Increase...	No...			None...
...enta Union,	5	4	34	1?			1 About same,	Yes,		Want of interest in parents,	Five...
...x Union,	7	7	51	4?	10		2 Prosperous.	No...	10	Want of interest in parents.	
...ville,	13	11	87	6?			Some falling off...				Three...
...ion,		6	70	4?			2 Prosperous.	No...		No...	None...
...ilmot,	8	8	80	70	2		Improving.	No...		No...	Twelve...
...sbyterian Church of Canada,		7	65	50	5		About the same.	No...			
...ne Ridge,	6	6	42	2?			Very prosperous.	No...		No...	Two...
...o, York, New Connection Methodist,	12	8	62	4?	4		3 Improving.	No...		No...	None...
...al Wesleyan,	8	8	8?	3?			Not much difference. ...	No...		No...	One...
...	21	18	17?	10?			15 Only four months opened.	No...		No...	Three...
...	24	2?	15?	10?	8?		3 Some improvement.	No...	3?	No...	Twent?
...		6	6?	4?	2?		3 Increase.	During winter.	10		Twent?
...s Union, Trout Brook,		4	6?	4?			4 Yes ...	During winter.	3?	Apathy in congregation.	Seven...
...Presbyterian,	10	8	5?	4?			15 Commenced July, 1856.			But much scattered population.	
...New Methodist Connection,	12	10	9?	7?	2		3 Stationary,	No...		Want of teachers,	None...
...esleyan,	12	13	11?	6?	14		16 About same,	No...		deficiency of teachers,	None...
...rry,	4	5	3?	2?			13 No remarkable change.	No...		Want of teachers,	Twelve...
...l New Con. Methodist, West District,	1?	12	16?	10?			2 Increase.	No...		No...	None...
...East District,	14	12	9?	6?	15		Two s s branched off.	No...	1?	Want of proper accommodation.	Twelv?
...Baptist,	6	5	5?	5?			1 New school.	No...		Apathy of parents.	Three...
...ilmot,			9?	6?			8 Similar,	No...		Many not in favor.	None...
...mall's Corners,	4	8	7?	4?	12		7 Prosperous.	During winter.		No...	Twelv?
...o Knox Presbyterian Church of Canada,	27	2?	21?	15?	20		3 About the same.	No...		Two Branch Schools lately opened.	Three...
...Zion Chapel,	3?	3?	2?	2?			4 More regular.	No...	3?	No...	Fifty...
...o American Presbyterian Church,	8	8	4?	3?	160		About same.	No...	1?	Want of male teachers.	None...
...Wesleyan Morning,	7	7	8?	5?	7		10 Great improvement.	No...		In efficient visiting committee.	Seven...
...Congregational Church,	3?	2?	2?	10?			6? Little difference.	No...		No...	
...Wesleyan Afternoon,	24	2?	16?	13?			3? Decrease.	No...	12	No...	Twent?
...Wesleyan,	3	3	6?	4?			3 Increase.	No...		Want of teachers,	None...
...sville,	3	3	3?	12	7		Prosperous.	No...	1?	Want of interest.	Four...
...	5	4	4?	3?			On the increase.	In winter.		Neglect of parents.	Three...
...land, near Martintown,	2?	12	4?	3?			4 Prosperous.	No...		No...	
...n Wesleyan,	19	17	16?	5?			Commenced six months ago.		4?		Four...
...al Presbyterian Church of Canada,	4	4	4?	3?			25 Very prosperous.	No...		No...	None...
...		7	4?	3?	12		3 About same.	In winter.		Neglect of parents.	None...
...Presbyterian Church of Scotland,	2	2	9?				4 Stationary.	No...			None...
...l Church of England,	16	8	8?	6?			5 Prosperous.	No...	1?	Want of general interest.	None...
...al Grifiltown Wesleyan,	10	9	10?				2 This our first year.	No...		No...	Six...
...Wesleyan,	19	18	24?	13?	3?		26 Better new. New school.	No...	4?	Want teachers	Very f...
...Grifiltown Wesleyan,	29	21	16?	11?			1 Prospered.	No...		No...	Twent...
...Elm Street Wesleyan,	1?	14	11?	11?			Recent formation.	No...	7?	No...	Six...
...po Wesleyan,		5	4?	3?			4 Increase. ...	No...		No...	None...
...ner Presbyterian Church of Canada,	14	9	7?	5?			3 In operation two months.	No...	3?	Irregularity of teachers.	Can't t...
...tle Presbyterian,	14	1?	7?	5?	7		4 Increase.	No...		No...	Eight...
...ho,	5	4	12?	8?			2 Yes, doubled.	No...		No...	Eight...
...and Wesleyan,	11	15	7?	6?			Same as last.	In winter.		Irregularity of teachers.	Twelv?
...lower Wesleyan,	7	6	3?	4?			4 Prosperous.	No...		No...	
...Hill,		8	5?	4?	14		Prosperous. Increasing.	In winter.	1?	Want of bibles.	Four...
...o,	8	4	6?	4?	1?		2 Yes, Increase.	In winter.		No...	None...
...ld Union,	2	4	6?	4?	14		First year of school.	Three months.			None...
...inburgh,	14	14	9?	5?	3?		Signs of improvement.	No...		Low state of church.	
...ity,	12	12	9?	6?	2?		15 Increase.	No...		No...	Two...
...al Presbyterian Church of Canada,	3?	12	20?	2?			16 Increase, 10 per cent.	No...	1?	Want sufficient number of teachers.	Forty...
...Richmond Street Wesleyan,	2?	2?	25?	18?	1?		24 Prosperous.	No...		irregularity of teachers.	One...
...o Wesleyan,		7	8?	4?			10 Compares favorably,	No...	9	Want of teachers.	Four...
...ville Wesleyan,	2?	10	11?	12?	1?		4 Increase. ...	No...		From partial neglect by teachers of prayer met'gs	Four...
...n Wesleyan,	4	5	2?	2?			5 Increase.	In winter.			Four...
...urham Union,											

many schol... ers of urch?	11. How many would not be under any religious instruction, were it not for the Sabbath School?	12. How many books does the Library contain?	13. Have you a regular Teachers' Meeting; and if so, is it for prayer, or for the study of the lessons, or both?	14. What is the average attendance at Teachers' Meeting?	15. How many, if any, were the conversions in your school during the past year?	16. Is your school in the habit of doing anything for Missions?	17. Are the people in your vicinity alive to the importance of Sabbath Schools?
	Very small proportion...	14	No.		None	Yes.	Not as desired.
	Fully two-thirds.	58	No.		Few.	No.	Part of them are.
	Perhaps half.	560	No.		Few.		
	Very few...	325	Yes, monthly, business.		Few.	Yes, 1856, £7 11s. 3d.	Many are.
	None.	45	No.			No.	
		80	No.		Few.		Yes, decidedly.
	Eight.	100	One for prayer.		Few.	No.	Considerable.
	One-third.	07	During summer, both.		Few.	No.	Not at all.
	Fifty.	150	No.		Few.	No.	Not fully.
	Fifty.	212	No.		None or of any.	No.	Not fully.
		14	No.		Few.	Yes, Missionary Box.	Not generally.
	Fifteen.	50	Yes, prayer and conference.			No.	Somewhat.
	One-half.	272	None ...		None.		Yes.
	Don't know.	80	None ...		Three.	Yes, Missionary Box.	Yes.
	None.	50	No.		Few.	No.	Only partially
	Seventeen.	225	No.			No.	Generally yes.
	About all.	106	No.		None.	No.	Yes.
	Forty-two.	25			None.	No.	Very few.
	Thirty.		None ...		None.	No.	Only a few.
	Fifteen.	82	No.		None.	No.	Only partially.
		26	No.		Few.	No.	They are not.
	Are seven miles from any church.	46	No.		None.	No.	Generally not.
	Five.	120	No.		None-Fear.	No.	Not generally.
		125	None ...		Few.		Very few.
		10	No.		Eight.	No.	Partially.
		100	No.		None.		
	About one-fourth.	850	None ...			No.	Yes.
	I think a great many...	174	Yes, for prayer.			Yes.	Yes.
		290	None ...	5	None	Yes.	
		20	Occasional, for prayer.		None	No.	Not as much as desired
	A few.	125	None ...		None	No.	Not fully.
	Sixteen.	180	No.		None	No.	Tolerably so.
		300	Monthly, for prayer; on Sabbath study lessons.		Five.	Yes, behalf of children of India	Some are.
		640	Monthly, for prayer; another for business.	10	Twenty-five.	Yes, collection each Sabbath.	Becoming more so.
	Twenty.	156	No.		Twenty-one.	No, but about beginning.	Yes.
	Uncertain	65	No.		None	Yes.	Partially so.
	Large portion.	98	No.		None	Yes.	Not.
	Can't say.		No.		Can't say.	Yes.	Partially.
	None.	420	Occasional, for study of lessons.		None	Yes, once a month.	Fear not.
	None.	100	Monthly.		None	Yes, £21 last year.	Three-fourths dead, one-fourth alive
	Twenty.	300	Yes, chiefly for consultation.		None	No.	Generally so.
	None.	124		12	Several	Yes.	Generally so.
	One-third	2	Semi-monthly, both.		Can't say.	A little	Not as would wish.
	Cannot tell if any.	175	No, occasional for business.	15	Many earnest	Yes.	Not as they ought.
	Cannot say.	230	No.			Yes.	Yes.
		100	No.		Two.	No.	Alas! no.
	None.	100	No.		None	No.	But a few.
		420	Weekly, study of lesson.	14		Yes, £20 P. C. Ms., £1 15s Knox Col.	Scarcely half alive.
	Fully one-half.	450	For prayer, monthly.	12	Two.	Yes, £18 15s.	Not particularly so.
	Cannot say.	1000	Monthly prayer and monthly business.	20	Six.	Yes, £18 15s.	I think they are.
	Most, if not all.		Monthly, for prayer.		None	Yes.	They are not.
	Ten.	60	Yes, every Sabbath, prayer.	11	Nine.	Yes, £15 p ann, extra occasionally	Partially so.
	Cannot say.	25	Weekly study, monthly business.	13	None.	Yes, £40 last year.	Yes.
		300	Study of the lesson.	15	Twenty-five.	No.	Partially so.
	None.	100	No.		None	No.	Think they are
	Can't say.	252	No.		None	No.	Not the least.
		252	Not frequent ...		Not known.	No.	No, not quite dead.
	Fifteen or twenty.	200	No.		One	No.	Generally,
		99			None	No.	Not sufficiently so.
		110	No.			No.	
	Many.	125	Monthly prayer, &c.		None.	No.	Generally so.
	One-half.	250	No.	17		Yes, Missionary Box.	Not very.
	Several.	700	No.		None	Yes.	Not much.
		48	Weekly, for both.		None	Yes, support orphan in India.	Not very.
	Cannot say.	350	No.		None	Yes.	Not as much as desired
	Can't say.	106	Yes, both.		Can't say.	Yes.	Not as much as they ought.
	Forty.	80	Prayer monthly.	11	Three.	Yes, £21 15s. 5d....	Not sufficiently.
	Forty.	100	Semi-monthly prayer and business.		Three.	Yes, £215.	
		600	Monthly, one each for business and prayer.		None	Yes, £215.	Yes.
	Thirty.	200	Monthly, one each for business and prayer.	14	Six.	Yes, £218.	Moderately so.
	Half.	200	None ...		None	No.	Some are.
	One.	300	No.				They are.
	Seven.	800	Yes, both.		Four	No.	To a certain degree.
	Two.	21	Yes, prayer and business.		None.	No.	Rather careless.
	None.	175	No, but intend to have.		Three	No.	They are.
	Twelve.	100	No.		None	No.	Yes.
	None.	154	No.		None	No.	Indifferent.
	One-fourth.	145	No.		None	No.	Yes.
	Twelve.	35	No.		Twenty-four.	Yes.	Yes.
	One-fourth.		Merely a business meeting.			No.	
	Twelve.	200	No regular meeting.		None	Yes, Missionary Box.	Many of them.
	Not known.	300	Yes, both.		None	Yes.	Yes.
	A considerable number.	710	One monthly prayer, 1 monthly business.	18	Nine.	Yes, £4 to Bible Society...	Not sufficiently
	Can't say.	450	Occasional, for business.	15	None	Yes.	Not enough.
	Fifteen.	400	No.			Yes, £22 15s. last year.	Yes, generally.
	Twenty.		Prayer and business.	12	Many seriously impressed.	Not regularly.	Not sufficiently.
			Monthly, for prayer.			No.	Yes.
	Fifteen.	40	No.			No.	Some are so.
	Forty.		Monthly, for prayer.			No.	Some partially so.
	Sixty-four.	40	Yes, every Sabbath, both.	11	One. Cannot say.	Yes, monthly.	Not sufficiently.
	Very few ...	350				Yes, £10 7s. 6d. last year...	A number are.

DESIGNATION OF SCHOOL. LOCALITIES. (Numbers in the left hand column refer to delegates, &c.)	1. How many teachers are there in your School?	2. What is the average attendance of teachers?	3. How many scholars are there in your school?	4. What is the average attendance of scholars?	5. How many of the scholars are over 15 years of age?	6. How many are under six?	7. Compared with previous years, is your school prosperous; and if so, what was the increase during the past year? —or otherwise what was the loss?			8. Is your school closed during any portion of the year?	9. Is it suffering from any particular cause?	10. How
								Loss.	Gain.			
Second Congregational,	10	7	37	24	...	...	About same.	...	...	No.	Want of teachers.	
Congregational,	16	...	...	...	...	...	Rather so.	...	...	No.	Suitable room. Lack of teachers.	
Wesleyan,	34	30	390	275	5	...	Very prosperous indeed.	...	125	No.	None.	Twen
de Gonzague, C.E.,	...	...	...	...	...	...	Sorry to say no.	...	...	No.	Want of interest.	
Congregational,	12	...	21	17	...	1	Increase.	...	16	No.	...	None
n Wesleyan,	20	10	100	65	...	...	Constantly improving.	...	30	No.	Want of ministerial encouragement.	None
lle Union,	6	5	50	30	...	...	Decrease. E. M. School opened.	...	...	No.	For want of zeal in parents.	Fifte
th School Section,	5	2	62	40	17	...	Increase.	...	10	In winter.	Tavern in neighbourhood.	Very f
Corners,	1	1	32	30	...	...	About same.	...	...	No.	Chiefly indifference of church.	None
	14	12	76	52	10	...	Increase.	...	16	No.	Lack of teachers.	Four
School Section 12, Union,	8	6	40	30	...	...	Quite prosperous.	...	...	Six months.	No.	Two
cond Congregational,	16	16	114	80	6	...	Yes it is.	...	20	No.	Non-attendance of parents.	None
mary, Presbyterian,	4	4	54	40	20	...	Prosperous.	...	...	No.	...	None
d,	8	4	50	36	15	...	About same.	...	...	In winter.	...	None
g,	5	5	32	22	...	...	Improving.	...	...	No.	...	
s, Gore,	12	10	90	72	20	...	Increase.	...	...	No.	More earnestness.	Nine
ion,	12	10	80	60	6	...	Prosperous.	...	4	No.	Want of teachers.	Two
	12	12	130	110	...	...	...	...	...	No.	...	
Church of Scotland,	12	10	60	40	20	...	Increase.	...	10	During five months.	None.	Four
	4	4	50	44	15	...	Much the same.	...	...	In winter.	...	Ten
le Christian,	4	4	41	30	...	...	...	...	...	In winter.	...	
	15	8	80	55	...	...	Increase.	...	...	No.	Principal want, teachers.	Seven
Presbyterian Church of Canada,	12	8	115	50	15	...	Decrease.	...	10	No.	Want of teachers and countenance of parents.	One.
, C. E.,	12	10	104	60	15	...	Increase.	...	...	No.	...	None
et Congregational,	5	4	64	60	...	...	Increase.	...	...	No.	...	None
St. Paul's Church of Scotland,	11	7	80	45	10	...	Decrease.	...	...	No.	Want of teachers.	None
United Presbyterian,	7	7	60	44	...	...	Stationary.	...	...	No.	...	None
on,	12	2	50	30	...	...	No perceptible difference.	...	...	No.	Indifference of parents.	None
nashan Union, 3rd Section,	16	12	100	75	9	...	Prosperous.	...	25	No.	It is from many causes.	
lle Methodist Episcopal,	4	4	50	30	10	...	Decrease.	...	...	In winter.	No.	None
a Wesleyan,	7	6	52	32	4	...	Prosperous.	...	...	No.	...	Ohio,
ale Union,	10	8	100	65	13	...	Increase.	...	24	No.	Want of teachers.	Eight
g,	10	8	50	30	4	...	Increase.	...	...	No.	...	One,
Union, Colborne Avenue,	12	10	75	50	16	...	Increase.	...	20	No.	No.	Four
nd Primitive Methodist,	No	numbers	given				Prosperous.	...	...	No.	...	
Primitive Methodist,	8	8	32	24	...	...	Prosperous.	...	...	In winter.	Indifference of parents.	Two,
Township, 2nd Con., Presbyterian,	4	4	56	40	...	...	Prosperous.	...	...	No.	...	None
nited Presbyterian,	5	5	45	25	...	...	Prosperous.	...	...	No.	...	One,
reek Union,	7	6	65	45	4	...	About the same.	...	...	One month closed.	Indifference.	None
esleyan,	10	13	122	75	2	...	Yes. Increase.	...	...	No.	Want of teachers.	Four
Wesleyan,	12	12	86	51	3	...	Prosperous.	...	20	No.	No.	None
h Union,	4	4	60	35	3	...	About the same.	...	...	No.	No.	None
Guelph,	7	6	41	30	5	...	About the same.	...	...	No.	No.	None
t Union,	7	6	60	44	...	...	Prosperous.	...	...	No.	...	
o Presbyterian Church of Canada,	15	13	45	45	...	...	Prosperous.	...	...	No.	...	None
Primitive Methodist,	16	6	35	20	9	...	Commenced November, 1856.	...	...	No.	No.	
t Front Presbyterian,	4	4	30	20	...	...	...	...	...	No.	...	
Wesleyan, Adelaide Street,	30	22	250	150	...	...	Much the same.	...	...	No.	No.	Twen
Yorkville,	27	24	140	121	20	...	Prosperous.	...	40	No.	No.	Twelve
Berkley Street,	12	11	110	80	15	...	Increase.	...	23	No.	No.	Seven
d Church of Scotland, St. Andrew's,	11	11	85	50	1	...	Prosperous.	...	20	No.	Yes, one.	
Wesleyan, Great St. James Street,	13	12	104	73	...	...	Increase.	...	20	No.	Yes, several.	Thirty
Cote Street Presb'n Church of Canada,	33	30	300	200	40	...	Prosperous.	...	50	No.	No.	None
Baptist,	11	8	72	40	...	...	Prosperous.	...	...	No.	No.	Three
Wesleyan,	...	...	50	50	...	...	...	...	...	...	...	
n,	23	20	163	130	...	...	Prosperous.	...	...	No.	No.	Fiftee
n,	7	6	60	40	...	...	About same.	...	...	No.	Energy in parents.	None
th, Kingston, Church of Scotland,	8	6	70	50	20	...	Prosperous.	...	...	No.	No.	Two.
oke Congregational,	8	5	45	30	...	...	About same.	...	...	No.	No.	
Wesleyan, Adelaide Street,	10	7	100	75	10	...	...	...	...	No.	...	None
United Presbyterian,	8	5	56	40	4	...	Decrease.	...	12	No.	No.	None
Bible Christian,	10	8	78	45	...	...	Increase.	...	...	No.	No.	Four
Presbyterian Church of Canada,	27	23	240	214	50	...	Very prosperous.	...	30	Yes.	No.	None
Wesleyan,	16	12	135	85	...	...	Prosperous.	...	...	No.	No.	Four
New Connection Methodist,	15	14	160	102	13	...	Prosperous.	...	33	Yes.	Want of good library.	None
Congregational,	15	6	170	120	...	...	About same.	...	...	No.	Apathy of parents.	None
burgh Union,	12	10	80	44	15	...	About same.	...	...	No.	Apathy of parents.	Nil.
rd Presbyterian Church of Canada,	6	4	43	31	5	...	Increase.	...	10	During winter.	Apathy of parents.	Two,
, C. E., Wesleyan,	6	4	49	30	6	...	Decrease.	...	...	During winter.	Want of unity and zeal.	None
rne, C. E., Wesleyan,	11	7	64	45	4	...	Decrease.	...	...	No.	None.	Twen
d Church of Scotland,	8	8	42	25	2	...	Increasing.	...	15	No.	None.	None
Wesleyan,	32	25	200	50	...	...	About same.	...	...	No.	Want of being open all year.	None
burgh Union,	11	5	42	30	30	...	Commenced November, 1856.	...	...	During winter.	Not aware of any.	Ten.
wn,	12	12	75	50	...	...	Increasing.	...	...	Two months.	No.	Nine
ton, C.E., Wesleyan,	11	6	64	50	...	...	About same.	...	25	No.	...	Eight
Township Wesleyan,	11	11	80	65	10	...	Increase.	...	10	No.	None.	None
Presbyterian Church of Canada,	6	4	50	40	...	...	...	...	14	No.	Priestly influence.	None
Presbyterian Church of Canada,	8	5	58	35	13	...	Decrease.	...	...	No.	...	None
xford,	19	19	54	43	...	...	Commenced May, 1856.	...	...	No.	...	
d Congregational,	15	13	65	60	...	...	Prosperous.	...	...	No.	None.	Five,
rn,	34	30	223	180	6	...	Prosperous.	...	...	No.	...	
non Wesleyan,	11	9	81	70	10	...	Only six months opened.	...	...	No.	...	

11. How many would not be under any religious instruction, were it not for the Sabbath School?	12. How many books does your library contain?	13. Have you a regular Teachers' Meeting; and if so, is it for prayer, or for the study of the lesson, or both?	14. What is the average attendance at Teachers' Meeting?	15. How many, if any, were the conversions in your school during the past year?	16. Is your school in the habit of doing anything for Missions?	17. Are the people in your vicinity alive to the importance of Sabbath Schools?
Twelve,	200	No,			Yes, weekly Bible Society,	They appear to value them,
Fifty,	150	Once a month, for both,	24	Fifteen	No,	Appear to be,
	100	No,			A good deal,	
None,	21	Yes, study of lesson,	2		No,	No,
Can't say	300	Occasional, for prayer and business,	4	None	No,	They are alive,
Ten	350	Only occasionally,	15		No,	No,
Five,	250	Occasionally,	4	Don't know,	No,	Small part only,
One-half	100	None,		None,	No,	Measurably so,
A good many,	250	No, no prayer meeting in Township,		None,	Yes,	Some yes, some no,
Twenty-five,	300	Monthly, for business,	5	None,	Yes, weekly collection	Far, far from it,
Eighteen	130	None,		Four,	Yes, £5 14s. last year,	No,
Many of them,	250	Prayer and business monthly, lesson weekly,	Good		Not regularly,	Becoming so,
None,	None	No,		Five,	No,	Yes, room for more,
	150	No,		Don't know,		In some measure,
						Not generally,
Thirty,	100	None,		None,	Yes,	Not sufficiently so,
Twenty,	1000	None,		One,	No, but in contemplation,	Not much, until recently,
	600	Monthly, for prayer,				To some extent,
A few,	150	Occasional, for school management,	6	None,	Support two Indian Orphans, &c,	Not nearly so much as should be,
	500	No,		Eight made credible profession	No,	Many are,
Twenty-five,	210				No,	Yes,
Six	100	Occasional, for business,	8	None,	No,	Very negligent,
Twenty,	200	None,		None,	No,	Much room for improvement,
Four,	300	Yes, for prayer,	10		No,	Are not,
Cannot say,	250			None,		
	300				Yes,	No,
	500	No,		None,	No,	
Twenty,	150	No,		Do not know,	Yes,	A few, but not generally,
Two-thirds,	300	No regular meetings,		Cannot tell,	Not yet,	They are,
None,	300			None,	Yes,	No,
Cannot say	140		7	One,	Yes,	Not equal to importance of work,
Twelve,	200			Several,	Yes,	Yes,
None,	400	None,		None,	Yes,	Yes,
Unknown	300	No,		None,	Yes,	No,
Six	150	No,		Two	No,	No,
Thirty,	150	Yes, for prayer, &c.,		None,	Doing much,	Generally,
None,	60				Yes,	Yes,
A number,	400	No,		Don't know any,	Yes,	Only a few,
One-half	187	No,	12		Have a Missionary Box,	Partially,
One-third	500	One monthly, prayer; one monthly, business,	10	None,	Yes,	Yes,
Most of them,	120	Lesson and business,			Yes,	Yes,
About one-third	200	Monthly for Prayer,		None,	Yes,	
	100					
Four,	100	Yes	6		No,	Yes,
A considerable number,	500	Not very regular for Business, regular for Pryr,			£37 last Christmas week,	Not sufficiently,
Very few	500	Prayer, monthly,	15	Not aware,	Yes,	Believe so,
Forty,	500	Prayer and consultation, monthly,	Po'rly		Yes,	By no means,
Twenty-five,	500	Prayer, &c., Monthly		Not any,	£7 last Christmas,	An unfavorable neighborhood,
Ten	690	Quarterly and occasional,	30	Thirty	Support two Orphans in India,	No,
Fifty to sixty,	690	Prayer monthly, and every Sabbath	11		£6 3s. 8d. last year,	Yes,
	590	Yes, for study of lesson		Two	£27 0s. 3d. last year,	
	400	Yes, both				They are,
Cannot tell,	315	We have both,	13	Fourteen,	Yes, monthly,	They are,
Fifteen,	50	No		One Teacher,	No,	No,
Being a mission school, many would,	200	Quarterly, School in country,	8	Believe two,	Support one orphan in India,	No,
Few, if any,	100	No				Not as should be,
	100	Both,			Yes,	Yes,
Twenty,	110	Study of Lesson weekly,	7	None,	Yes,	Very much so,
A large portion	250	Monthly business, weekly lesson	14	Cannot tell,	£19 9s. last year,	Yes,
Have no idea,	150	Yes, prayer and business	8	Don't know,	Yes,	Not much,
	150	Monthly for business	15	Don't know,	Yes,	No,
Not many	350	Yes, for prayer,	12	Don't know,	Yes,	
Very few	100	None for some time				They are not,
One-third	300	None,		Cannot say,	£4 last year,	No,
One-half	400	No,		None,	No,	No,
	150	Prayer and business	7	None,	Yes,	No,
	500	Business and mutual improvement	12	None,	No,	Careless and indifferent,
None,	250	No,		None,	No,	Cannot say they are,
Can't say	220	No, but intend to have		None,	Yes,	To some extent,
Thirty,	50	No, but intend to have one		None,	Yes,	To a certain extent,
	80	No		None,	Yes,	Generally they are,
Fifteen or twenty,	400	No		Nine,	£15 annually F. C. Mission,	Seem not,
	80				Yes,	Yes, but want more life still,
Four,	120	No			Support an orphan,	Think they are,
None,	400	No		Look for fruit,	Last year £4 17s. 0d.,	Some are, not all,
One-half	200	No		One,	Not yet	Not as much as could wish,
Fifteen,	800	Not regular		Six,	Yes, Bible Society,	Feeling favorable,
Fifty-three. (No. of Bohemian child'n at'g sch'l.)	70	Monthly prayer		None,	Support two orphans in India,	Not so much as they ought,
Thirty,					No,	
	67160					

RECORD OF THE PROCEEDINGS

OF THE

Sabbath School Teachers' Convention,

HELD AT KINGSTON ON THE 11TH, 12TH AND 13TH FEBRUARY, 1857.

WITH APPENDED

STATISTICAL AND OTHER INFORMATION.

Published by Order of the Convention.

Montreal:
PRINTED BY JOHN LOVELL, AT HIS STEAM-PRINTING ESTABLISHMENT,
ST. NICHOLAS STREET.
1857.

The adviseableness of holding a Convention of Sabbath School Teachers in Canada was suggested by Mr. S. J. Lyman, at a Meeting of the Committee of the CANADA SUNDAY SCHOOL UNION in July last. The Committee approved of the suggestion; but, as only a minority of the Sabbath Schools in Canada co-operated with the Union, they hesitated to take any decided action, believing that, to be successful, the Convention would require to be Provincial, and that it would not be so if they alone moved in the matter. It was agreed, however, to appoint a sub-Committee to invite an expression of public opinion in relation to it.

This was done, and it led to a preliminary meeting of a few gentlemen from different parts of the Province, at Kingston on the 25th of September last. The decision at that Meeting, in favor of the Convention, was unanimous; and a local Committee, consisting of the Superintendents of Sabbath Schools in Kingston, and a Committee of arrangements, consisting of the original sub-Committee of the Union at Montreal, were appointed, and the Secretary of the latter was instructed to correspond with parties in Toronto, which city was unavoidably not represented at the Meeting, for the purpose of inviting the organization of a co-operating Committee there. The friends in Toronto who had previously manifested a warm interest in the movement heartily responded to the call.

These three Committees carried out, as far as possible, the views expressed at the preliminary meeting.

With the exception of the superintendent of the Great Western Railroad, the managers of all the roads applied to, liberally entered into the plans and views of the Committees and proprietors of newspapers throughout the Province as liberally inserted the notices sent to them.

From time to time the Committees were much gratified by the apparent growing popularity of the movement: a popularity not to be ascribed to their efforts, but to the over-ruling Providence which blessed their labour, and which ultimately gave to the Convention a measure of success which far exceeded their expectations.

May the same Divine grace accompany this Report, and give to all who read it deep and abiding impressions of the importance of Sabbath Schools, and resolution and ability to labour unceasingly for the spiritual good of the youth of our country.

CONVENTION OF DELEGATES

FROM

SUNDAY SCHOOLS IN CANADA

AND

REPRESENTATIVES FROM THE UNITED STATES.

WEDNESDAY, 11th Feby., 1857.

Conformably to the arrangements of the local Committee, delegates assembled in the Wesleyan Methodist Church, Sydenham Street.

At half-past 9 a.m. the Rev. Mr. Marling called the Meeting to order, and proposed Dr. Mair, of Kingston, as temporary Chairman.

Nomination approved.

Dr. MAIR accordingly took the Chair, and called upon the Rev. Mr. Lauton, to open the meeting with prayer.

After which Dr. MAIR said, that he did not think it necessary to read the circular by which this Convention had been called together. It was sufficient to say that it had originated in a committee appointed to meet in Kingston, for the purpose of considering its expediency. Three committees were named, one for Montreal, one for Toronto, and one for that city, and the result was manifested in the highly respectable meeting then before him. It afforded him the utmost pleasure to be called to the position he then held; and he would remark that he had been much struck the day before with the remarkable intelligence and good countenances of the numerous Delegates who had arrived for the purpose of attending the Convention. He had lived in countries where he had become familiar with very different faces. He had been in N. S. Wales and Van Diemans Land, where he frequently had to encounter persons of the very worst characters, and could state it as a remarkable fact that crime stamped its impress on the countenance. Having had these opportunities then of observation, he could not help comparing the benevolent and intellectual faces before him with those of men who had been familiar with crime, and with everything else which tended to make the heart worse than it naturally was. He cordially entered into the desires expressed in the prayer just offered, and had no doubt the Convention would tend greatly to the advancement of the cause in which all were so much interested. He felt, too, that the Lord would be present with them. It was delightful to reflect that there were present men who merged all their differences in love—love to God—love to Jesus—love to the Spirit of Truth and Holiness. Would that the day might shortly be seen when all men, of all the various opinions which were entertained, would come together to advance the cause of the common Lord. In the large correspondence which had taken place on this subject, he thought that there was but a single letter in which the writer ventured so far as to oppose this movement, "because this Convention would consist of rather heterogeneous materials." That he (Dr. Mair) could not understand. Heterogeneous! He took it the materials were quite the reverse. Had they not one Father?—one Saviour?—one Spirit influencing them all? How, then, could the body be heterogeneous? They were all one in Christ Jesus. To these few remarks he had only to add, that it was his duty to call for the appointment of a temporary Secretary.

MR. GEO. HARCOURT, thereupon nominated Mr. J. W. TAYLOR, of Montreal, and he was appointed to that office.

MR. S. J. LYMAN, then moved the appointment of a nominating Committee to nominate officers, and the Chairman named

Messrs. S. J. LYMAN, Montreal.
" D. BEADLE, St. Catherines.
" GEO. HARCOURT, Toronto.
" JOHN PATON, Kingston.
" W. BEGG, London.

The committee retired, and devotional exercises were engaged in for half an hour.

The nominating committee having returned, reported the following names for the officers of the Convention, and the nominations were unanimously adopted, viz:—

HON. JAMES FERRIER, President.

VICE-PRESIDENTS:

* Rev. R. V. ROGERS, Midland District.
* Mr. J. S. SANBORN, M.P.P., Eastern District.
Mr. WM. BEGG, Western District.
Dr. JOHN MAIR, Kingston.
Mr. Sheriff TREADWELL, Ottawa District.
Rev. WM. LANTON, Prescott.

SECRETARIES:

Rev. JOHN SCOTT, Bath.
Rev. THOS. HODGKIN, Doon.
Mr. J. W. TAYLOR, Montreal.

---

* These gentlemen were not present. The Nominating Committee put their names on the list of officers, as it was understood that they would be present.

The Hon. JAS. FERRIER, having taken the chair, spoke as follows :—

Christian Brethren: I have repeatedly during the course of my life occupied positions of honor and responsibility, but never before have I felt myself so highly honored, nor have I occupied so responsible a position as I do this day, in presiding over this large and deeply interesting assembly of delegates from Sunday Schools, East, West, North and South. Were we met in this place to determine what course to pursue in reference to some great political question affecting the material interests of Canada, how many eyes would be on us! how many would be ready either to censure or applaud the decisions at which we might arrive! But it is for no such deliberation we are called together. The purpose of our meeting is to consider whether more cannot be done in our Sunday Schools to give to the children of this Province a more thorough Bible education; and if this Convention should, during its present session, devise means superior to those now employed in the conducting of our Sunday School work, or if it should excite a stronger feeling in the breast of every delegate in this house, so that we may return to our schools with redoubled energy to teach the rising generation the knowledge of the truth as it is in Jesus, the end will be fully answered.

Sunday School teaching will, in my opinion, increase the prosperity of our rising country to a far greater extent than any political question which has ever occupied the attention of our Legislature; and it is capable of effecting what no purely secular education can effect, viz.:— the establishment of that high moral and religious character, without which there can be no security to either person or property. Gentlemen, I feel deeply on this subject; and I believe that the future destiny of our country depends on the sound religious and moral training which our children receive in the Sabbath School. Let us for a moment look at our Province, divided as it is into two classes—the Protestant and Roman Catholic, and let us note the difference between them, which we attribute to the effects of the Bible. We Protestants believe that God has given us the Bible as his revealed will; that he commands us to read and obey it: and that it is our duty to teach it to our children and all around us. To the Roman Catholics the Bible is a closed book—they are prohibited from reading it, and the result is lamentable in this country as well as on the continent of Europe. I point to these facts to show that the present and future prosperity of our Province depends on the thorough Bible education we give to our children. And I would ask—where are they to get this? The District Schools do not furnish it; neither do the other schools established for secular education; and, therefore, we have to look to our Sunday Schools as our only hope, and we expect, by promoting their interests, to attain the desired end. For ever shall I thank God that I was born in Scotland, and that in the school where I was educated, there were a Bible and a Testament class. But, gentlemen, when we consider that not only the temporal prosperity, but the eternal destiny of every human being depends on his being made savingly acquainted with the glorious plan of Redeeming mercy revealed in the Bible, and when we remember that so large a portion of our race die in youth, is it not our duty to teach the children of our Province to read that " God so loved the world, that he gave his only begotten Son, that whosoever believeth in Him should not perish, but have everlasting life ?" Our children must read that Jesus came from heaven to earth to save them. They must hear of the love of Jesus to children when on earth,—how he took them in his arms and blessed them. Where, I ask, can this be done so well as in the Sunday School? For about thirty years past, I have been teaching or superintending Sabbath Schools, and during that time, I have seen the glorious effects of Bible truth on the minds of children. I have seen them die happy in the prospect of spending an eternity with Jesus, who said : "Suffer little children to come unto me," I rejoice to be able to report to this Convention, that in the school of which I am at present the superintendent, there have been, during the past year, about thirty young persons converted to God, and that in Montreal, our prospects of further success are brighter than they ever have been.

Gentlemen, a great deal has been done, and is now doing, to furnish a liberal secular education to the youth of our Province, and no one can be more anxious than I am to secure this. But let us never forget that the sciences do not teach the way of salvation. Mathematics will never solve the problem—how can a sinner be justified before his offended God?— nor can mental philosophy ever show that the carnal mind is enmity against God. No! in the sciences, whether physical or metaphysical, there is no voice which tells us of the height, the depth, the length and the breadth of the love of God to man. To the Bible, therefore, and to the Bible alone, let us go, and take with us the children and youth of our land, that from the study of that Book of Life, teachers and children may be made wise unto salvation.

After further devotional exercises :—

Mr. S. B. Scott moved that the President do appoint a Business Committee. Carried.

The Chairman named—

Rev. F. H. Marling,	Rev. Geo. McDonald,
" J. Elliot,	" J. Shortt,
" A. Bullard,	Mr. James Walker,
" W. Jeffers,	" S. B. Scott.

Mr. J. W. TAYLOR moved, and it was resolved, that the roll be made up, and in doing so, in order that delegates may become known to one another, that each rise in his place, announce his own name, the name of the School he represents, and the name of the place in which it is situated.

Roll of delegates present taken accordingly.

The Rev. MR. SMART, after announcing his name, mentioned that he represented the oldest Sunday School in Canada, it having been founded in 1811, whereupon it was moved, seconded, and carried unanimously, that the Rev. Mr. Smart be the first Vice President of the Convention.

Rev. Mr. Smart thanked the meeting for the honour conferred upon him. He little expected when he arrived in Canada, forty-six years before, to see such a day as that. It was indeed an honour to be made their first Vice President; but it was a still greater one to have been permitted to be the founder of the first Sunday School in Canada. He believed that both the person and the labours of the late Rev. Mr. Osgood, were known to most of the brethren, but he might inform them perhaps, that Mr. Osgood was inoculated with Sunday Schools in Brockville. He came there as an Itinerant missionary in 1812, and he was so pleased, that he began immediately to travel through the Province and to establish Sunday Schools wherever he went. For his own part, he (Mr. Smart,) ought to erect his Ebenezer and say, hitherto the Lord has helped me. He came to Canada forty-six years ago, and he might say that the Lord had now made him two bands—two bands! why what a number of bands were present that day! He thanked God for the preservation of a very feeble life and constitution till he saw that day, and especially till he saw that the cause of Sabbath Schools had taken such deep root in Canada. That cause was identified with the moral and political, he might say even with the scientific and literary progress of the country.

Mr. Thompson (Rochester) said he would present Mr. Smart with a portrait of R. Raikes.

The Business Committee reported the following recommendations, which were adopted.

1st. That the hours of meeting be from half-past 9 to half-past 12 in the morning, and from half-past 2 to half-past 5 in the afternoon, and that the first half-hour of each Session be spent in devotional exercises.

2nd. That no speaker speak more than once or occupy more than ten minutes on each subject, without permission of the Meeting.

3rd. That all business come through the Business Committee.

4th. That the following questions be discussed in their order, and that not more than one hour be devoted to each.

1. What is the best mode of training Teachers for Sabbath Schools?

2. What ought to be the necessary qualifications of Teachers before their appointment to Sabbath School classes?

3. Can the giving of rewards be so conducted as to be of advantage to the scholar, and to the prosperity of the School?

The Business Committee further recommended.

1. That a Committee of five be appointed to make all nominations required by the Convention, and that the said Committee consist of—
Messrs. S. J. Lyman, G. H. Delter, W. Burns, Ainsley and Dayfoot.

2. That a Committee of three be appointed to examine the statistical returns with the view of completing them as far as possible, and preparing a summary thereof to be submitted to the Convention.

3. That a Committee of three be appointed to make up a statement of the expenses of the Convention, to ascertain the probable cost of publishing the proceedings, and to report a plan for raising funds, the said Committee to be called the Committee on Finance and Publications.

All of which recommendations were adopted.

On motion it was resolved that all communications to the Convention be referred to the Business Committee.

The proceedings of the morning were then closed by prayer by the Rev. Mr. Smart.

SECOND SESSION.

The Convention assembled again at half-past two o'clock; and after a hymn had been sung, the Rev. Mr. Burpee offered prayer. Another hymn having been sung, the Rev. Mr. Scott prayed.

The minutes of the first Session were read and confirmed.

They led to a statement, that the first Sunday Schools in Lower Canada were established in Montreal and Stanstead in 1816; the latter school having sent out a missionary who was one of the first to go to the Sandwich Islands, and whose labours had been blessed by God to the conversion of many hundreds of souls. It was founded by Mr. P. V. Hibbard.

The Nominating Committee submitted a report which was accepted, naming for the

COMMITTEE ON FINANCE AND PUBLICATIONS:

Mr. H. A. Nelson, Chairman.
" James Stewart.
" H. T. Croty.
" W. J. Morris, and
" John Barnard.

AND FOR THE COMMITTEE ON STATISTICS:

Mr. Alex. Macalister, Chairman.
" George Hagar.
" F. T. Pearson.

They also reported the names of speakers for the public meeting to be held in the evening, viz:—

Rev. J. Shortt, Port Hope
Rev. B. W. Chidlaw, Cincinnati, Ohio.
Rev. M. Miller, Ogdensburgh.
Rev. C. W. Denison, Buffalo.
Rev. A. Bullard, Boston.
Mr. D. P. Janes, Montreal.
Mr. J. D. Foote, Buffalo.
Mr. T. H. Thomson, Rochester.
Mr. E. T. Huntington, Rochester.

The Business Committee recommended that the third question on the printed list in the circular calling the Convention, viz:—

"Are Sabbath Schools at the present day accomplishing the purpose for which they were instituted? viz: the religious enlightenment of uncared for children? Has this not been in a great measure departed from by giving more heed to the children of the Church than to those who are without means of religious instruction, and would not their usefulness be increased by a return to the original object"? be put second on the Docket, and that the third topic be,—How can we gather into our Schools the thousands of children who now neglect them? and that the topics previously named as 2nd and 3rd, be placed 4th and 5th respectively.—Adopted.

The question "WHAT IS THE BEST MODE OF TRAINING TEACHERS FOR SABBATH SCHOOLS," was then taken up.

The Rev. Mr. SMART (Brockville) said, that from an experience of forty-three or forty-four years, which was about the length of time since he became a Sunday School teacher, he had come to the conclusion, that the best mode of improving teachers was by their frequently meeting together and holding cordial Christian communion on the task in which they were engaged. That was the plan which had been adopted at the Fitzroy School in London, with which he had been connected, and where there were 490 or 500 children. The teachers assembled at six o'clock on Sunday morning to converse, and to lay their feelings, and difficulties and encouragements before each other, so as to perfect their plans for the extension of the gospel through the school. He had attempted to carry out the same plan in Brockville, and so far as it was tried it had been very successful. Indeed if there was anything that could cheer the heart and mind of the old man who addressed them, it was the retrospect of those times. He could not tell the number of missionaries and ministers who had gone forth from the Fitzroy School. The Morrisons, Gordons, Milnes, and many others had however begun their career in it. And so it was at Brockville. There the teachers had more time than in London, and they met once a week to converse among themselves, and once a week to converse with the children round a table. There had been not less than six or eight ministers go out from that school, and he believed its success was chiefly owing to the intercourse of which he had spoken. This was one means and though not the only one, was a very important means of training teachers. One great defect in the lives of Christians in this country was the want of communication between themselves. They heard a sermon, good, bad, or middling, and then left the Church for the week; but they did not rally round each other; nor become acquainted with each other as they should do. Neither were the ministers sufficiently acquainted with their people, for they were generally very deficient in visiting. The same thing was true of Sunday School teachers.

Mr. RUTHERFORD (Peterboro) conceived that the chief difficulty of carrying on Sunday Schools was found in procuring properly qualified teachers, and this question of training was, therefore, of the very highest importance. Long connected with Sunday Schools, the last four years as a superintendent, he knew the difficulty well. In Peterboro, they had found the best plan for meeting this trouble was to form a class expressly for the purpose of educating Sunday School teachers. In that place, they had found that adults, not being the masters of their own time, did not make the best teachers, for family ties frequently kept them away from the school. Besides, men advanced in life had

not generally had the same advantages of intellectual training as the young men who were growing up. But by establishing a Bible Class, many young persons, who were not likely soon to leave the school were interested in its operations. What had been said already was very well; but he thought the first thing was training. At Peterboro, they had an excellent class for teachers many of whom continued in the school, and better than all, became converted.

Mr. MORRIS (Perth) remarked that the Scotch Church School to which he belonged had adopted the same course, and it turned out that teachers thus trained always took more interest in the school than those who had not been thus educated.

Mr. HETHERINGTON (Melbourne) acquiescing in the views of the previous speakers, recommended moreover the plan he had seen adopted in Lower Canada, of discussing beforehand the lesson which was to be given out on the coming Sabbath. At the meeting for this discussion the minister took the chair *ex-officio*, and the teachers having given their sentiments upon the topic in hand, the minister corrected them if he observed any thing erroneous in their views. Thus all were prepared to give instruction to the children. There were several ministers who were first taught in that school.

Mr. BEGG (London) believed it was of the greatest importance, especially in Union Schools, that the teachers should be better instructed in the best modes of teaching their classes. It was easy to get persons to attempt to teach; but it was not easy to secure that interest in the work and qualification for it which were required. In London, under the direction of his pastor, there was a large Bible class for the training of the teachers; and he held that it was the duty of the pastor thus to train the young of the flock. Any one who did not meet the Bible or some similar class once a week, did not do his duty. Besides the Bible class, his pastor was in the habit, during six months of the year, of meeting the teachers one night in the week, and going over the lesson of the following Sabbath with them, giving them all the information in his power upon the doctrines embraced in the lesson, or upon the illustrations of the country, or manners of the people which might come up in reading. This could not be done in country places where the ministers resided at great distances; but in such cases his place might be taken by the most intelligent teacher.

Rev. Mr. JEFFERS (Montreal) thought a resolution should be passed recommending, that in connection with every Sunday School there should be a Bible class taught, either by a minister or some other competent person, which class should be made subservient to the objects of the school, and that as part of the regular work of the school there should be a male and female Normal or Training School, out of which the teachers for the Sunday School might be selected. He therefore moved :—

Resolved, That with reference to the training of teachers, it is desirable and earnestly to be recommended, that, when practicable, there be maintained in connection with each school a Bible class for teachers, and such elder and more advanced scholars as are invited. The said class to meet once a week. And that in addition thereto, there be also maintained as normal training classes, out of which teachers may be taken when wanted a superior class for each sex, composed of the elder and more advanced scholars. Such classes to form part of the school, and to meet at the same time and place as the school.

Rev. Mr. MILLER (Ogdensburg) conceiving the great object of Sabbath School instruction to be the leading of the pupils to Christ, held that none but those who knew Christ by the teaching of the spirit could be fitting instructors to guide others to him, who is the way, the truth and the life. It required John to teach that it was the Lamb of God which taketh away the sins of the world. As the first step, then, towards bringing out teachers it was necessary to go to the only place whence fitting instructors could come—to the foot of the cross. The first question to candidates for admission to the Church should be not only, do you know Christ; but, are you willing to labor for him? If so, we can take from that class those who are to teach. As to Bible classes, the universal experience of the Church corresponds with the reason of the thing, that such classes must lead to the prosperity of the Sabbath School. In Rochester, Bible classes had been established with the understanding that those educated in them were afterwards to be employed in Sabbath Schools, and, indeed, he thought that all members of Churches should understand the importance of preparing themselves to instruct others. The most gifted colporteurs had come from the Sabbath Schools, and one who had labored in Canada had been taken to the school by his child, and he thence went forth to spread abroad the lessons he himself had learned. The most useful missionaries and servants of God in other ways were those who had been brought into the Church from the family altar under the influence of Bible classes and Sunday Schools. He had heard many say when introduced into the Church late in life, that their old habits of thought still clung to them. To have good teachers, then, let them go to the schools, let them look out for the child whose eyes sparkled while the teacher spoke to him of the love of Jesus, and when such a one had been fixed upon, let him be followed up and trained for the purpose to which he was to be persuaded to devote himself. One reason why some Churches were blessed in having many ministers go out from them was, that their Sunday School teachers thus set their minds on children, who were to be teachers and ministers.

Mr. NORMAN, (King) thought the excellent speeches just made did not touch the real point. If some schools were not to exist before they could get real converts for teachers, it would be long before they flourished much. In a neighbourhood where there was only occasional preaching, sometimes on Sunday evenings, and sometimes on week day evenings, a Union Sabbath School had been started, and he did not suppose it would be easy at present to find a more moral, civilized neighbourhood. Now there was no whiskey consumed there, though formerly there could be no "Peace" without grog. At present none was used in the shanties, and on Sunday mornings, there was a full house though no pastor. He had no professing Christian near him; but the young men and women were growing up to respect and practice morality, and he hoped that in another year he might have something still better to relate. God answered prayer, and he wanted the inhabitants of large cities, where they could choose their teachers, to pray for the people in the backwoods. In the meantime let them say whether a school was to be broken up because real converts could not be obtained for teachers. The question had been long upon his mind; but he thought when people could not do what they liked, they ought to do what they could. At the school he spoke of, they had a library of 300 volumes. As to training, of course, it only could be thought of for the young. It was impossible to train those who for twenty years had been running about all day on Sundays visiting and tale bearing.

Mr. ADAMS (Montreal) remarked that Mr. Jeffers had a large congregation, and it would be easy to work among them; but in the small organization with which he (Mr. A.) had to deal, the strict rule contended for would not work at all. He had been obliged to do the best he could to get teachers, and often did not know whether he would have to stop or go on. He must take just such timber as he could get—a converted teacher if possible, if not, one of good moral character, otherwise the school must be abandoned. If he wanted to interest a young man or a young woman in the scriptures he got them to take a Sabbath School class, and thus he imposed upon them the necessity of studying the bible. He knew a case of a boy who had been at school; but got too large to stay there. He accordingly left and spent his Sundays in perambulating the streets; but one day he went past the old Church, and the minister happening to see him said: "George suppose you take a little class this morning?" He did so; he was asked to take it again, and he became a very consistent teacher.

Mr. GEMMILL (Toronto) thought they were wandering from the point, which was the training of teachers. If a resolution like that recommended by Mr. Jeffers passed, the elders and pastors training the elder children in conformity with it would provide exactly the sort of teachers which Mr. Norman required in the backwoods. Men would go out and do the work of Sunday Schools where no converted men could now be found. His experience was that it was easy to appoint teachers but not easy to keep them with their classes, and this not because they were not Christians, nor because they did not wish to do good; but because they did not understand how to communicate their ideas to the minds of the young. That showed the importance of training.

Mr. THOMPSON (Rochester) gave his brother from the backwoods the right hand of fellowship. It was easy to make plans for cities with Churches and Church members; but his brother was right. He said, do what you can. Let him go home not to tell the people to shut up the schools till they could get converted teachers for them; but to pray that these teachers might be converted. At Rochester they at one time had no converted teacher at all; but they had thirty-five unconverted ones, of whom every one was brought in. Afterwards the Church separated, and they had again sixteen unconverted teachers, and they were all brought into the Church. He recollected the last, the day after he was converted making a record in his own hand : "Blessed be God, I am the last of the teachers of this school ; but I too have found mercy." He would rather have an unconverted teacher with some go ahead, and zeal, and ability, than a converted one who could not or would not do any thing at all. Let his brother go home ; keep his schools going, and pray God would bless him. It was impossible that he should not. Children would not go there, and read the bible, and yet not be converted. They must either be converted or leave the school. Let his brother go back and light a flame that would set all the back woods on fire.

Mr. STEED (Sarnia) had heard a good deal about schools which, he supposed, all belonged to Churches. His, however, was in a different position, being a Union School. There were three to six clergymen in the town, and they never interfered with it. Perhaps they did not wish to go out of their own fields. At any rate, the conclusion he came to was, that it was necessary to make the school self-sustaining, and raise teachers for themselves. If they had not the means to get up good Bible and training classes, they must do the best they could. Perhaps other teachers would say their schools had as little support as his. For his own part, he thought it the duty of clergymen to give their support to the Union Schools.

Mr. DUGGAN (Kingston) stated, that his Church had a Bible class, conducted by the Pastor, and a teachers' meeting every Tuesday evening, at which, after prayer, the lesson for the following Sunday, announced on the previous Sabbath, was taken up and considered. The teachers read the lesson, verse by verse, and the pastor gave his views upon it. The teachers then asked each other their opinions. This with the Bible class and one other thing, had been mainly instrumental in securing teachers of the right kind. The other thing was prayer that the young in the school might receive the truth.

Rev. Mr. HODGSKIN (Doon) held that teachers should be able to interest their classes, and this not only by the possession of knowledge, but also by ability to impart it. Without that, the scholars could not be made to feel that they attended school with profit to themselves ; and they therefore could not be retained under the influence of the school. In his experience, he had found that the bread of life must be cut very small, and served up very nicely, in order to interest the child ; and ministers should remember when they went to the schools, that they were no longer preaching to their congregations, but had to take the children and talk to them all. He believed that teachers sometimes thought that they were not teachers, but ministers preaching. He remembered seeing a Bible class conducted by a person who, he thought, believed himself very well qualified. He was a person of some note, and had called the land after his own name. This person thought it would be well to have his (Mr H.) brother, two years younger than himself, as his scholar. The lesson was in Jeremiah, where it is said : "The days come saith the Lord, that they shall no more say,—The Lord liveth that

brought the children of Israel out of the land of Egypt," and the teacher asked,—why it shall no more be said, the Lord liveth? He (Mr. H.) saw his brother sitting and trying to look grave. He was the last in the class, and when it came to him, he said he did not see that that was in the book. "Oh, yes," said the teacher, "they shall no more say, the Lord liveth." His brother told him to read on a little, and he would see that the blessings in the day which was foretold, were so far to exceed those that had been granted to the children of Israel in the land of Egypt, that the former deliverance would be forgotten in the greatness of the latter. "Oh, well," said the teacher, "we will ask no more questions to-day ; read on, if you please." Now, he (Mr. H.) thought, if the truth, conveyed in the passage, had been fully impressed on that man's mind and heart, he would not have made so miserable a spectacle of himself. To make schools respectable, then the teacher must be able to make himself respected.

Mr. HAGAR (Montreal) mentioned, that in the school with which he was connected, there were several adult or Bible classes. The elder scholars did not leave the school, but grew up in it ; and when old enough to do so, took part as teachers. From the Bible class, in the past year, several teachers had gone out to supply branch schools, and when the superintendent wanted teachers, he could always apply to these adult classes. The members of these Bible classes sometimes took turn to lead the classes, and they thus prepared themselves and became qualified for teachers. In his own class, several had lately been taken for regular teachers in the school.

Mr. McALLISTER (Kingston) said that 204 schools had reported, in which there were 2040 scholars over sixteen years of age, so that many teachers might be expected from them.

A DELEGATE here recommended as a kind of manual, a book called the Teacher Taught.

Mr. BEGG (London) would like to see the nomination of a Committee of Pastors to recommend books for the instruction of teachers.

Rev. Mr. DUGGAN especially counselled teachers to adopt a holy walk and conversation, example being better than advice.

Dr. MAIR (Kingston) on this account was very anxious that teachers should be punctual in their attendance at school in order to insure punctuality on the part of the children.

Mr. STEWART (Kingston) remarked that the population in this country being very fluctuating the children were usually but a short time under the instruction of their teachers. For that reason the teaching should be concentrated, and instead of going through the whole bible, truth should be presented in as condensed a manner as possible. Now where teachers were not converted they were unable to give that kind of instruction which was so essentially necessary. He could not conceive how an unconverted teacher could present the Lamb of God which taketh away the sins of the world, or how such a person could be a living epistle of Christ. It was no doubt often impracticable to get men of the stamp required ; but there should be nothing in the resolution which would seem to lose sight of the necessity of having such persons if possible.

Mr. McKay (Montreal) said that in the school with which he was connected, the teachers met every Sabbath morning at 10 o'clock, for one hour, for prayer and the study of the lesson. To this meeting the elder scholars were often invited; few, however, availed themselves of the privilege. He approved of what Mr. Gemmill had said, and thought the plan hinted at a good one, as it had a tendency to fit those who attended for profitably engaging in the work of teaching, and was one—among many—of the means blessed in preparing the young for taking classes in the Sabbath School. All the qualifications alluded to were essential; but *gifts* were required as well as *graces*, and the liberal education of the young was not only desirable, but should on no account be neglected.

A DELEGATE thought that Bible classes should not be formed merely for the teachers. There should be such classes for all the scholars likewise. Then each one would show what ability he had, and the best qualified teachers would be picked out from the whole.

The RESOLUTION moved by the Rev. Mr. JEFFERS, having been seconded by Mr. AYLESWORTH, (Odessa,) was read by the Secretary and carried.

The Convention then took up the next question :—

ARE SABBATH SCHOOLS AT THE PRESENT DAY ACCOMPLISHING THE PURPOSE FOR WHICH THEY WERE ESTABLISHED ? VIZ : THE RELIGIOUS ENLIGHTENMENT OF UNCARED FOR CHILDREN. HAS THIS NOT BEEN IN A GREAT MEASURE DEPARTED FROM BY GIVING MORE HEED TO THE CHILDREN OF THE CHURCH THAN TO THOSE WHO ARE WITHOUT MEANS OF RELIGIOUS INSTRUCTION, AND WOULD NOT THEIR USEFULNESS BE INCREASED BY A RETURN TO THE ORIGINAL OBJECT ?

Rev. Mr. JEFFERS (Montreal) said that, when Robert Raikes first collected his Sunday scholars and put them under a female teacher, he did so with the intention of instructing the poor and destitute only, and he understood that the question now under discussion was whether that idea had not been greatly lost sight of, and whether Sabbath Schools were not now devoted to other purposes than collecting the ignorant and destitute? Certainly this was not kept so much in view as it was by Raikes, and he thought it was a subject of gratitude that the Sunday School operations had been extended over more ground. The Bible Society had been formed in the first instance to give the Bible to the people of Wales ; but it could not be said that it was losing sight of the original object because Bibles had been sent elsewhere. God had made use of Robert Raikes' idea and had caused the Sunday School to become the nursery of the Church, enabling the Church to carry out the mind of Christ in the educating of her children. The uncared for should be helped. But placing the original idea too prominently in the foreground would, in his opinion, do harm instead of good, and he was not very friendly to that spirit in some Christian organizations which kept constantly in mind that they were intended for the poor and ignorant. Such words as ragged schools and poor schools showed, perhaps, a bad spirit in those Christians who thus named them.

Sunday Schools ought rather to be considered as a part of Church organization and the work of the Gospel.

Mr. S. B. SCOTT (Montreal,) read the following paper :—

That Sunday Schools to a very great extent at the present day, are not fully accomplishing the object for which they were designed, and in consequence, are not accomplishing the good they might do is believed from the following :

Sunday Schools were originally designed for those who were destitute of religious instruction.

Sunday Schools now are principally devoted to those who have, independent of the Sunday School, every desirable opportunity for the acquirement of religious knowledge.

Sunday Schools now are made up mostly of the children of the church, who, if they are not, ought to be faithfully and prayerfully instructed at home.

In view of these facts we may inquire, what is the effect of present Sunday School operations upon members of churches and their children.

Before the days of Sunday Schools, a large proportion of christian parents strictly and regularly attended to the spiritual training of their households, deeming this as much a part of the work God had designed for them to do, as it was to provide for necessary daily food.

Is this the case now ?—

So far from it, that evidences are to be found in almost every house, that this duty which had been strictly performed by religious families, from the days of the Prophets to those of Robt. Raikes, has been either partially or entirely laid aside, as being no longer useful.

It is to be feared that but few christian parents *now* feel the importance of this duty as they would were there no Sunday Schools, and though doubtless there are some who as they should do, look upon Sunday School instruction only as a help to their own, at the same time it cannot be doubted, that a *very large portion*, and many believe *by far the largest portion* of the members of the church, entirely neglect the religious training of their children. And why ?—Because they have come to the conclusion, that this is the legitimate work of the Sunday School, though by what command or example in the Bible, this transfer of so important a duty is made, it is not easy to discover. The effect too upon the children of this class of Christians, is most surely very much to their disadvantage. Not that anything is chargeable to the unfaithfulness of the Sunday School Teacher, for if there are faithful devoted spiritual minded *Christians* any where, they are to be found in the Sunday School ; but really how much time does the Sunday School teacher have, however faithful he may be, to devote to his class during the whole week ?—On an average not more than 30 minutes. And what too is the portion of Sunday School Scholars, who as attentively listen, even during this small portion of time, to the instructions of a person comparatively a stranger as they would to the earnest words, gushing from the full heart of the father or mother. We are also forced to conclude, that by the present system of Sunday School operations, vast numbers of christian parents, for *want* of the mental and religious exercise God has designed for them in fitting themselves for the important duty of training up their children in the way they should go, become weak and useless members of the Church, and their children barely exist upon the crumbs they receive from others instead of growing upon the bountiful supply God has provided for them.

It is a common and with many a favourite remark, that the Sunday School is the nursery of the church, because that now the larger portion of those added to the church are from the Sunday School, and in consequence the Sunday School is credited with their conversion.

How far this matter *should* be looked upon in *this light*,—is a subject of much doubt.

It is true that now most of the additions to the Church, are from the Sunday School, but it is also true, that nearly all of these, are the children of Christian parents.

Now what is the fact in relation to conversions in this class of persons *before* the days of Sunday Schools. There is no reasonable doubt of there having been as great a proportion of these persons added to the Church, before Sunday Schools were established as there has been since, so that really the only perceptible difference is, that *now* the individual goes round through the Sunday School, into the Church instead of direct from home as before.

This may lead us to inquire, what good after all are Sunday Schools now doing?

And humbling as the answer must be, we are forced to the conclusion that they are not accomplishing by far so much good as we had supposed.

It is the firm belief of many good men, that Sunday Schools are really eminently useful only in so far as they are instrumental in the salvation of those who are in the main, destitute of all other means of religious instruction.

It is true that they may be, and in some cases doubtless are a help to Christian parents in instructing their children, but the value of this agency, in these cases, is so small in comparison with the great opportunity for their usefulness in the right direction, that really it is hardly worth mentioning.

That there is in our midst, a class of persons, destitute of all moral and religious training, is believed by all, that there is a *large* class of such persons is believed by many, but all who have taken the trouble of informing themselves upon this point, are perfectly astonished at the result of their inquiries.

In the city of Brooklyn, New York, a place noted for zeal and energy in efforts for destitute children, there were about one year since 15,000 Sunday School scholars, 30 of their schools being Mission schools, and yet at the same time it was estimated that there were in that city alone 20,000 children out of Sunday Schools.

It is also worthy of notice that at the Sunday School Convention of the State of New York, held at Albany a few days since, the alarming statement was made, that there are *now*, in that single State, not less than 300,000 children, whose moral training is totally uncared for, except as they may be reached by the Sunday School. Compare the population of Canada, with that of the State of New York, make all the deductions required on account of those who are catholics, and of course apparently beyond our reach, and we have here in Canada the vast number of not less than 100,000 to 150,000 of this same class of destitute children.

It is to be feared that we have allowed ourselves to fall into a grievous error, in relation to the uncared for in our midst.

While throughout the Province of Canada the number of children *out* of Sunday Schools, is vastly larger than that of those who are *in*, we have criminally closed our eyes to their deplorable condition. We are literally surrounded by darkness and heathenism. Those very persons who are to be men and women, and active upon the stage of life, at the same time with our own children, are growing up in ignorance of the Bible, strangers to God, profaners of the sabbath day, and eminently qualified for all that is sinful and wicked.

And those very persons whom God has designed, as instruments in his hands, to rescue them from this fearful condition, are to-day almost as totally regardless of their welfare, as if their existence was merely in the imagination.

But it is a question not lightly to be thrust aside. Is there not a fearful responsibility resting upon us in relation to them? To-day they are within our reach, and they may be gathered into Sunday Schools and taught the truths of the Bible, but in a few years it will be with them as it now is with those who are, apparently, entirely beyond the reach of our efforts. If it is in our power in any way, or by any means to bring them, or any number of them, under the influence of the gospel, I ask dare any of us take upon ourselves the responsibility of withholding the means God has provided for the accomplishment of this purpose?

What Sunday School teacher, after having carefully reflected upon this subject, and knowing as he comes before his class next Sunday, that there is not one in it, in whose father's house there is not bread enough and to spare, can feel in his heart, that he is really and faithfully accomplishing the object and design for which Sunday Schools were established.

I think we must conclude that the Sunday School is designed for the destitute, for those against whom every other door of access is closed, and I feel that until all these are gathered in and provided for, we have no business whatever with those for whom God has provided Christian fathers and mothers, only as they may be made useful in attracting or influencing others. We ought by no means to lose sight of one important fact in connection with this subject, which is this, that wherever or whenever any successful effort has been made for this class of persons, it has been done through the agency of the Sunday School.

We have every reason to believe this to be God's own appointed way of accomplishing this work ; for look where we may, we see how, in every place and at all times, when this kind of instrumentality has been used with a firm reliance upon Him for His blessing, invariable success has been the result.

Who can estimate the amount of good that would be accomplished—the joy and rejoicing that would be in heaven—if the efforts which are being made by all the Sunday Schools in Canada for the benefit of the children of the Church, were directed to those who are now in ignorance of the Bible? Where is the sin in my disbanding my class, convinced as I am that they are doubly provided for, (though I may love them as my own children,) and sending them home to be cared for by their Christian parents, while I go into the streets and lanes, and gather into the Sabbath School the children of the irreligious, the Sabbath breaker, the drunkard, the infidel, and the outcast? and, in this way endeavour, by all the influence I have, to give food, spiritual food, the bread of life to those who are perishing; and, on the other hand, am I not incurring the displeasure of heaven, by continuing, as I do, the teacher of those who should be taught at home, to the neglect of those who are sure to be lost, if *this* effort is not made for their salvation? Where is the benevolence which has reason to expect God's blessing upon efforts to provide food and clothing for the rich? He that giveth to the rich shall surely come to want. Who would think of sending Bibles and Missionaries to England or the United States, leaving Burmah and Africa to perish? and yet, are not our present Sunday School operations, to a large degree, of a similar character to this?

We often feel, and sometimes express much anxiety in relation to the matter as to who are to fill the places of the great and the good men who are now occupying stations of influence and importance upon the stage of life. Is not the inquiry of vast importance, too, who are to fill the places of those who now occupy the cells in our jails and penitentiaries? Who are to occupy the places of drunkards in their poverty and in the gutter? Who are to occupy the places of thieves and pickpockets, and all the other pests of society? The places of all these are to be filled, and that too, no doubt, by some children who are in our midst. They are now in the Sunday School of the devil—a school in which they are receiving the most perfect education—and it will not be the fault of their teachers, if they are not more eminently qualified to fill their various positions than those who are before them.

I may be in an error, but it is my firm belief, that the destinies, for time and eternity, of thousands of these most unfortunate beings depend upon the action and results of this Sabbath School Convention; and I dare not close without urging my Brethren here assembled, to look well to it, that the blood of these perishing souls is not found in their skirts in the great and final day of all things.

Mr. Carman (Matilda) differed materially in opinion from that of the last speaker. To pass a resolution in the sense of this paper would be to destroy the Sabbath School cause. The effect it would produce in the towns and villages could not but be unfortunate. Every man desired to be considered better than his neighbor, and if it were said that schools were established merely for uncared for children, the children who were really uncared for, but whose parents would not admit that they were so, would be driven away from such schools. He had sometimes asked himself, if a school should not be made, separate from the rest, for the wandering children of the streets; but he soon · saw the impropriety of it, and that as everybody had a desire to be thought to belong to the upper classes, no one would like to send their children to such schools. The teaching of poor children was one of the grandest objects of the Sabbath School; but one of the greatest attractions for them was, that they would be there gathered together with the respectable children of all classes of the community. He would make one remark that seemed appropriate to this subject, this was that a serious evil in Sabbath Schools was the love of expensive and gaudy dress. Nothing was more calculated to drive children away than to see the teachers coming equipped in tinsel and finery, and nothing was less becoming those who professed to be followers of the meek and lowly Jesus.

Rev. Mr. Shortt (Port Hope) remembered an occurrence at Port Hope, where the people were and are particularly loyal. It was desired to commemorate the Queen's marriage; and in order to do so it was arranged upon the proposal of a gentleman who had his head full of old country ideas, that a dinner was to be given to the respectable poor, and those of the respectable poor who applied were to have tickets for the dinner. But not one applied, though it was to be supposed that there were poor people in Port Hope as well as elsewhere. So it would be with Sabbath Schools. If there were to be respectable poor schools, no one would enter them. Just in the same way a Temperance Society which professed to be a society for reclaiming poor drunkards would be a failure. All the respectability that could be obtained should be procured, and if possible he would like to have the Governor General for a most worthy grand patriarch. Another consideration: all professing Christians should educate their children in a religious manner; but that was not practically the case, so that many such children were as much neglected as the most uncared for. Therefore, it was the business of those concerned in Sunday Schools to collect alike the most respectable and the most destitute.

Mr. Thomas, (Clairville,) after expressing his happiness at thus meeting Protestants of all denominations in Canada, declared himself of opinion that it was neither doing good to our fellow men, nor serving the cause of God truly to make schools only for the destitute and uncared for, he thought one reason why hundreds more children were not brought into the schools in days past was the fact, that such schools had been always more or less sectarian,—adapted for children of this, that or the other Church. The school he was connected with, however, was a Union School, and the teachers came from the different denominations. It was a large school for a country place; but there had never been a word of regret on account of this arrangement, and if all schools were conducted on the same plan, the way to advance the good cause would be made plain. Let all meet on the broad principles of truth and they would be mightily edified, and if any teacher advanced something which was not in accordance with the mind of all, it would be a pleasant thing for them to meet and talk it over so as to conform themselves to the truth as it is in Jesus.

Mr. Becket (Montreal) offered a resolution recommending the establishment of visiting committees in connection with each school.

Rev. Mr. HODGSKIN moved that the third topic on the docket be combined with the one now being discussed, and that the time for their consideration be extended to the hour of adjournment.

The motion was seconded by Mr. Hetherington and carried.

The words HOW CAN WE BEST GATHER INTO OUR SCHOOLS THE THOUSANDS OF CHILDREN WHO NOW NEGLECT THEM, were therefore added after the word OBJECT.

Mr. BECKET thought his resolution covered the whole ground.

Rev. Mr. MARLING (Toronto) believed that to put up over schools : " For uncared for children," would prevent any parents from sending their children. What parent would admit that he did not care for his children ? He wanted, however, to hear their American brethren on this matter, as they were understood to have taken a great deal of pains in it.

Mr. BECKET (Montreal) thought his resolution did nothing like proposing to put up " For uncared for children." The object of obtaining visiting Committees was to bring in children. If all the children were brought what more could be wanted ?

Mr. ARMSTRONG approved of the resolution, having seen the good working of visiting committees, who, in his school, were called absentee visitors. A year and a half ago that school had dwindled down to the number of sixty, of whom the average attendance was about thirty. Four persons were, therefore, appointed to act as visitors, to get all children not connected with other schools to come to that one. That plan answered well. In order to get children who were uncared for, it was not necessary to write that over the door. He was Superintendent and made no distinctions. The child who was capable of being in a particular class was placed there. If there were absentee visitors appointed to all schools, a large number of children now uncared for would be brought in, yet nothing invidious would be done. He had heard it said, that the children themselves made the best missionaries ; but believing that the great object of Sabbath Schools was to bring children to the knowledge of Jesus, he thought they could hardly be expected to take the same interest in bringing other children to the school as was to be looked for from persons engaged in the service of the schools, especially when these last were so engaged from high and pure motives.

Mr. THOMPSON (Rochester) had seen a great deal of effort put forth to get into the schools children who did not belong to any Church unless the Church of Rome, and had seen these efforts blessed ; but it was no particular machinery that did it. It was the love of God shed abroad in the hearts of those who labored, and though at first there were many little difficulties, it was found at last that the parents could be got at. He knew a brother who really had but one talent, but that one was the talent of trying to do good. He tried to get the French Catholic boys into the school. Fathers and mothers and priests all opposed him, but he succeeded. He was a mechanic, and used to go down to the residences of these poor people,

sometimes with firewood, at others with bread or clothes. They found he had a heart, and he thus came to exercise great influence over them. He (Mr. Thompson) could bring tears into the eyes of either parents or teachers by the mere mention of the name of that brother. He did not approve of putting up " poor schools." He once saw an arrangement where there was an infant school, and a Sunday school, and one called an intermediate school, which was devoted to the poor children who were picked up in the streets. He told the friends that this intermediate school would break down, and, in fact, it ran down to nothing. His desire was, that all the children should come together to the same school. They were all possessed of immortal souls, if they had not all clothes. Let the poor children be taught that they have souls, and the rich that they should respect the poor on that account. Committees for visiting were all very well ; but that would not do alone. He had known a young lady who taught in a mission school ; but on a wet Sunday her mother said she had better not go as it was at a distance, and as the mother thought she would find no children there. He (Mr. T.) said she had better go ; she herself insisted on going, saying she was sure she would find her children. On her coming back he asked if she had had any scholars ? " Yes, seven as usual, she always had children." The reason was, that she always went herself. Let the teachers take an interest in their scholars and the children could not be kept back.

Mr. MORGAN gave an account of the manner and difficulties of getting up a school at Dickinson's Landing. When he first went round, the parents said there were schools enough ; but he insisted that they should have a Sunday School, and he at last collected forty-five children to start with. He next went round to collect for a library with he started with $14, and he had now 250 volumes. Then there were difficulties with the children. Some would say they could not come to school because they had no shoes. He said you shall have shoes, and he got them for them. In ten years they had only lost about nine Sundays from having no school, and when some difficulties had occurred, he insisted upon losing no more. He was a poor shoemaker ; but when the Convention was talked of, he said he wanted to go and show himself and see what was going on, and bring good news back from it. At present he was fireman to the school. He had been several years a trustee as well ; but when they turned him out of that he insisted on keeping the other office, and so he made the fires still.

Mr. FOOTE (Buffalo) thought that Committees would do little to get children to the schools. Give him one little boy or girl zealous in the work, and he had yet to see the place where children could not be prevailed on to come to the school. He had a large file of correspondence on Sunday Schools, and every letter complained of want of teachers. There was no trouble about getting children. He had visited one place where there was a Christian Church, supposed to have great efficiency ; but there were from 300 to 500 neglected children there. He appealed to them on this subject, and three weeks after on returning there, he was told that a little Irish Catholic girl had done more than all the Church to collect scholars. With respect to poor and uncared for children, he thought those parents who cared for their children at the present day were the exceptions; but he certainly did not charge that on the Sunday Schools, there were other influences which made parents remiss, and he feared that without Sunday Schools, the children of the Church would often be as much neglected as the children of the poorest parents.

Rev. Mr. Bullard (Boston) had labored for twenty-six years in this cause, and had heard nothing more frequently presented as a cause of regret than that parents threw off their responsibility on Sabbath Schools. But the schools ought not to bear the blame. In the early history of the United States, it was common for all persons religious or not religious, to attend to the instruction of their children, and in 1642 there was a law passed, that all persons should catechize their children and apprentices on Sundays, in the doctrines and grounds of religious belief—not of any particular belief. This was the law passed by the General Court of Massachusetts; but he doubted if the Court would entertain a proposition for such a law at present. Indeed as time advanced, it was found that all parties neglected the instruction of their children, and then the Sabbath School cause had to provide for the deficiency. These schools were in his opinion, great blessings even to godly parents; but in truth, few parents even among those who attended churches were professors of religion, and all the rest had children dependent wholly on the schools. As to neglected children, he would bring them into the schools to sit side by side with the rest. In the Broome street school, Boston, the question had come up two years before, shall we get up another separate school, or bring these children into our own school. The last plan was determined on, and a school of three hundred children was collected, half of them taken out of the streets. In the Infant school there were one hundred children, of whom all but fourteen were from the streets. The pastor's daughters went into the streets and brought them in. They then gave up the school to some men, and went out and collected another school. They had one school for adults with ten Swedes in it, eight of whom were converted, and thus learned the language of Zion before they learned that of the United States. He knew of one instance in which two classes, one of boys and the other of girls, were appointed to look for and bring children into the schools. In Manchester they appointed similar classes of young men and women. The men got fourteen and the women thirty four or thirty five; for the young women could always do more than the young men, and he knew one place where the calculation was that a lady was worth 13½ gentlemen. At any rate, the superintendent, a lawyer now in practice at Boston, soon reported a school of 530. The same thing might be done in Canada. It was a work in which pastors and teachers might take part, and both plans might be employed. One course was to propose to very little children to give them a book a piece, if they would bring in a scholar. In that case a little girl, perhaps, would go to her mother saying the teacher says, he will give me a book if I can get a scholar. How could the mother help going? The schools in the States had many scholars besides the children. In one church out of 530 members, 512 were in the school. The members of the better families were wanted to make teachers; but others were wanted to come and learn, and perhaps these last would eventually make the best teachers. In the meantime the little girl and little boy sat by the side of the adult scholar. At one of the towns in New Hampshire, it was determined to give one bible to whoever would bring in the most scholars; but there were two little girls, and one young man, each of whom had done so much that a bible had to be given to each of them. He saw this young man sitting in a pew with the little girls, and he took him for the teacher, till the Pastor came forward and said, here is a bible to be given to the little girl who has got twenty scholars; the other is for the other little girl who has got fourteen; and there was one for that young man who had brought in twelve young men, and though in thus acting he had been in opposition to his own set, he was not ashamed to come and sit with the little girls and to receive a bible as a present for what he had done.

The time for adjourning having arrived the final decision was deferred till the next sitting. The Convention, after singing and prayer, adjourned to meet at the City Hall at 7, p. m.

THIRD SESSION.

PUBLIC MEETING AT THE CITY HALL.

The President of the Convention took the Chair at 7 o'clock.

After devotional exercises, the President called for and introduced the Speakers in succession.

Mr. Thompson (Rochester) said he had never made a set speech in his life, and would not begin in his old age. He had been a Sabbath School teacher forty years, and had seen that God had poured forth his spirit upon these schools like rain upon the mown grass. In Rochester they kept a record of what occurred in the Sunday Schools, and without such a record, a school was not what it ought to be, and when teachers or scholars were united with the church the fact was entered. In the year ending January 1st, sixty-five scholars had been united to the church, making in all 655, to say nothing of those who had gone all over the land and made profession in other places. Yet very little had been done for God, though he had blessed that little. But if men would but try to work for God, God would bless them. Try!—that was the word every teacher and scholar ought to have written on his heart. It was the word of Raikes—"I will try." Montgomery had said of this work.

"Once by the River's side
"A little fount it rose,
"Now like the Severn's rushing tide
"Round the wide world it flows,
"One Heaven directed mind
"Reveuled the simple plan;
"Now, in the glorious task combined
"Ten thousand are one man."

He had asked a large manufacturer of buttons to make a Sunday School button with Robert Raikes' head and the word "Try" stamped upon them. If a boy had such a button as that, it would make a new boy of him, for as a remembrancer it would stimulate him in the performance of duty. Many had tried, and tried hard; but let them go back and try again. There was enough power here to convert all Canada, if all did what they might do. One thing he particularly desired, was, that the children should be taught to do good. One of the richest men in New York State, who had once been ready to hold a sixpence so hard as to make a hole in it, but who had got over that, had said to him. "Teach your children to give." If that were done, oh what an overflowing Treasury the Lord would one day have! Sometime ago his school began educating children in India, and when difficulty occurred he asked his children whether they would like to send the Indian boys and girls back to heathenism. The reply was, No. The heathen children then in question had been taught; the school where they were instructed broken up; and the children of his school now gave their money for the establishment of other schools. He knew a boy who went to school at three years old. He began with penny contributions. At four years old, he was prevented from attending school for forty weeks, at the end of which time he came to the school with forty cents in his pocket which he gave. He had now been twelve years in the school; but he never forgot his penny contributions. It was all moonshine, what some said, that the child should give only for his own school. They should give for the good of mankind. At his school, they had a library of five hundred volumes, and from time to time they said to the children, now who is for giving this library to the children where they have none. They all get up at once.

He had said that day in the Convention that he would present a daguerreotype portrait of Robert Raikes, to the venerable father who had founded the first Sunday School in Canada in 1811. That was forty-six years ago. Well, the Temple took forty-six years to build, and this father had been forty-six years building up Sunday Schools. He should now make him a present of the portrait of Robert Raikes.

Mr. Thompson accordingly handed the portrait to Mr. Smart, repeating the following lines:—

" Think how he taught unmoved and ardent
"In those sacred halls. Nor end his labours here,
" But onward rolled a mighty stream of rescued souls,
" To bliss, and joy supreme in heaven.

Rev. Mr. Smart, (Gananoque) expressed his thanks for the present, and after reminding the audience of the saying of Archimedes that he could move the world, had he a place to plant his machinery, remarked that the Christian had not only the machine; but a firm foundation whereon to plant it, the machine was education, which already nearly realized the wish of George the Third, that every child should know how to read, and every child who could read should have a bible. The bible was indeed the foundation on which the machine was planted, and the world, intellectual and moral, was already moving.

Rev. Mr. Miller, (Ogdensburgh,) conceived that men might already see before their eyes the fulfilment of the promise, that the hearts of the fathers should be turned to the children, in the spread of Sunday Schools, that peculiar enterprize of the nineteenth century. The importance of it was easily shown. In the Methodist Church, the aggregate increase last year was 80,000, which was almost the precise number of those who had been added from the Sunday Schools. The rest only sufficed to supply the places of those who dropped off by death. The experience of the Presbyterian Church was similar. During the last ten years, of every thousand received as communicants seven hundred and fifty were from the children of the church, and were united to it before they were twenty-five years of age. Only one in a thousand was added after sixty years of age. What volumes of exhortation in these facts, to remember the children! In his church, out of a hundred and ninety-nine applicants, of whom one hundred were by profession of faith, the largest part were from the children of the church. He would add to his friends motto "I'll try" the words "and persevere." Phidias, the sculptor, being unjustly banished from that native country where his statuary graced the Pantheon, repaired to Elis, far from the land of his fathers; but there he undertook to accomplish a work superior to any he had hitherto achieved, and presented to the world, the statue of Jupiter Olympus. Look at him thus toiling on the shapeless mass, to gratify his ambition and revenge for the injustice of his countrymen! But Sunday School teachers had to do with immortal spirits. On them they were to make their mark; and should they not persevere? In a school where severe rules for the preservation of order had been enacted, a boy was reprimanded by his teacher and by the superintendent, and told that he must be banished unless he reformed. Frequently the teacher impressed this simple lesson upon him. At last he was banished; but the lesson was constantly ringing in his ears, till at last it was the means of introducing him to an extended sphere of usefulness, first as a Sunday School teacher, and then as a superintendent who succeeded in building up many Sunday Schools.

Mr. Janes (Montreal,) had begged the Committee not to put his name on the list of speakers, and when they insisted and refused to take it off, he declared he would not occupy the meeting for two minutes. One of his reasons was, that he was very diffident and afraid to hear his own voice and the other, that his friends said his notions were very ultra, by which, he supposed, they meant they were exceedingly right, and he, therefore, dared not risk mischief by what he might say. But if it would do any good to hear something of his experience he would say this :—He had been more than thirty years in the Sabbath School as teacher, one of the visiting committee, and superintendent; and lastly, as teacher of the adult classes, and if he were asked whether he loved the work as well as he did thirty years before, he would reply: vastly more. His heart was never more thoroughly interested, nor more in the work than at that moment.

Mr. Huntington (Rochester,) would give a few statistics of the school of which Mr. Thompson had spoken. They had a book containing biographical records of the school, with the autographs of every teacher and scholar for twenty or thirty years back. It contained three thousand biographical sketches, and his colleague who had already spoken made it his business, if he saw anything in a newspaper, or anywhere else, of one of their scholars or teachers to insert it in the book. Whenever a scholar emigrated to the West or elsewhere, a record was made of the fact, and the collection was well worthy of examination. The school contained 430 scholars, of whom 140 were over fourteen years of age. It had young teachers and teachers who were fathers. Among the elderly teachers was the oldest man in the Church. With one or two exceptions that teacher had been in his place regularly for three years. One young lady had assumed the instruction of the female bible class in 1853 ; but her health became impaired and she was called to her resting place. On her dying pillow she had the consolation of believing that save one, all her scholars had been converted. As an evidence of what one little boy could do, he would mention that in Western Kentucky a reward was offered to boys who should bring in scholars. The first person that one of these boys applied to was his father. The man said " I dont know how to read." " We will teach you said the child." The father followed his son ; sat on the same bench by him ; learned to read; became converted ; and finally was sent out as a colporteur. At the end of four years he had established four hundred Sabbath Schools, and 35,000 children, within seven years were, by his instrumentality, gathered in. That boy was now a missionary. In New York, there were about 500,000 children and about 200,000 of these were in Sabbath Schools Among the rest were the Catholic children who went to their own schools, and it was proposed to adopt a plan to bring them all in. In the City of New-York, a good deacon and a Scotchman met a few little boys on Sunday morning for the sake of giving them instruction in the scriptures. Mr. Pardee proposed one day to visit him and see if he could render any assistance. At the appointed time Mr. Pardee went and found his friend engaged with ten or eleven boys ; but he had noticed on his way some boys who were playing at marbles. He asked if these had been invited ; and was told that they had been but would not come. Upon that he went out and found a lad thirteen years of age and other smaller boys together. He said to the elder. I have a motion to make and if you will second it, I think I can carry it —it is that you adjourn your meeting and go to the Sabbath School. " No" said the boy " I sha'nt do that." " Well" said Mr. Pardee, " you are doing two things that are wrong,—one is gambling, and the other breaking the Sabbath. I protest against them." "Oh come along boys" said the eldest, and off they went a little further and resumed their game. Mr. Pardee returned to the school, obtained a little book with pictures, and got a boy to accompany him. Then he approached the group again, reading the book to the boy and looking at the pictures. The other lads became interested and approached to see what the interesting story

was about. At length the eldest boy was left alone and he came up too. Then Mr. Pardee asked if they did not all want books, saying that just such were given to the boys at the school, and addressing the elder boy, now, said he, if you go all will go. " Oh, he knew that," he said, and then " well boys I lets all go to school." They went in ; but the eldest boy soon slipped away, returning however, soon after with the exclamation—" here Mister—here are some more boys." He slipped out again, and returned in the same manner, so that before the school broke up he had gathered sixty four boys ; and he was then made assistant superintendent, and ultimately he became much interested in the work. He was taught the trade of machine manufacturing in the Southern part of Connecticut, and if any of his hearers should ever read of Casper Howard, that was the boy. In one of the largest schools in Brooklyn lately, a man came and asked the superintendent for a place to teach a bible class. Dr. Morel did not know if he had any place to spare. " Can I have that corner ? " " Certainly." Next Sunday he had five young men ; the next as many more, and at the end of the year forty were converted from that class. The reason he (Mr. H.) was so much interested in Sabbath Schools was, that he had had no pious father or mother ; but he went to Sabbath School. All the children of the family were converted by those schools, and after that, the parents were converted likewise.

Mr. Foote (Buffalo,) loved Sabbath Schools, because through their agency, he had seen communities of Sabbath breakers and drunkards transformed to fearers of God and lovers of righteousness ;—because they promoted the interest of the Church, the country, the father, the child, the scholar and the teacher. He was sorry to hear any charges brought against them.

" Earth had no name more worthy fame.
" The countless blessings it had shed.
" Would be revealed when worlds were fled."

The Sabbath School did not get credit enough. You might indeed look to a particular school, and see no fruit for the moment; but where was that seed prepared, of the germination of which they had heard that night ? In the places where those who had toiled and sowed in tears, twenty or thirty years before, leaving the generation that came after to gather the harvest ; and long after the accounts of those now labouring should be sealed up, the value of their work would be better understood. There were in this land hundreds of thousands of neglected children ; but the past history of Sabbath Schools warranted the conclusion, that they were powerful as a remedy. Go to Afric's shore, and there would be found, borne thither in a ship from other lands, the boy who had been trained in a Sunday School to love Jesus Christ. He went to tell to those benighted minds the way of salvation. The missionary there, too, began with the children. This had once excited the wonderment of an old Chief who met a missionary, and asked : " What is this you come after—the children ? " Yes," said the missionary, "I come to do you good. The old people are hopeless ; but my hope is with the young, and we must first get their affections." " Ah ! " said the old man again.

"You are crafty; you want to get possession of our country, and to live long." "No; I expect soon to die; but I came to tell you of Christ's salvation. Bye and bye, your countrymen will fear God, keep the Sabbath, and have only one wife." "Ah!" repeated the old man, "you will live long and get the world. The child to-day is the man to-morrow."

Rev. Mr. Denison (Buffalo,) had had some trouble to come, but had done better than some of his brethren, for he had brought his wife with him; and without saying anything about women's rights, he would add, that she had come as a delegate. He felt that the friends of Sunday Schools might well congratulate their wives and daughters on the aspect of the Sabbath School cause, both here and in the United States. In both countries, everything which had been achieved was owing to their Christian women; and if ever either country fulfilled the destiny which he believed God had in store for them, it would be because of the exertions of the Christian mothers, and wives, and sisters. It was not enough that children should be taught in the Sabbath School—their mothers must take them on their knees, and there teach them to pray — must have their closets where they might take their little ones as Samuel of old to Samuel's God. When he thought of the Christian union manifested that evening, his heart rejoiced. Perhaps one brother was a Presbyterian. He was a Baptist; but if the Baptists were close communionists, they felt in close communion with all others who were concerned for Sabbath Schools; nor were there, he believed, any people who went together more steadily shoulder to shoulder, in the education of the young, than the Baptists of the United States. They knew that if they could instruct the children aright, it would be impossible for any tyrant to forge his chains for them hereafter. The American brethren felt united to their Canadian friends, and felt the necessity of this union, not only because they recognized the differences of denominations, but also of nationalities. There were a great variety of Saints,—St. George, and St. David, and St. Andrew, and, last of all, St. Jonathan; but with all this diversity, there was only an imaginary line between the true Christians of Canada and the United States. When he crossed the Suspension Bridge, he thought of that; but he must confess the line there was rather a lofty one. But when he listened and heard the great diapason of thunder which went up to the heavens from that cataract, he reflected that it ascended alike from the shore of Canada and that of the United States. Americans, then, need not ask Canadians whether their thunder was louder than their own, or which side poured over the most water; but each might hear and see without jealousy the cataract which belonged to the other, and the same thing was applicable to the Sabbath School Union. One thought had occurred to him, which he would mention. It was the dignity of being a Sunday School Teacher. There were young ladies and gentlemen who said:—"Well, about this Sunday School teaching—this getting half a dozen boys and girls on to a bench, with a testament and question book—is it not rather undignified?" But here was a fact. The Chancellor of the University of New York, Theodore Fre-

linghuysen, one of the ripest scholars and best Judges in America, at seventy-two years of age, is a teacher in a Sunday School. Mr. Pardee, a gentleman whom, if they all knew, they would all love, a very extensive merchant, was now engaged in the work of building up Sunday Schools; and he mentioned that, having once asked a friend, what induced him to be a teacher, he received for a reply:—"Because it is so dignified an occupation to teach the immortal mind, and because I love it." Mr. Pardee asked again:—"What capital do you represent as a broker?" He was told, $6,000,000 per annum. Yet that man, with such large concerns on his shoulders, sat down every Sunday in a little school, with a company of ragged children. Let the rich men of Canada say what they thought of that. Was not that man fulfilling his mission in putting the stamp of God on the youthful mind? The manner in which that gentlemen tried to keep the children round him, was by studying four or five hours a day everything novel and interesting; collecting facts and incidents to please his pupils. It often happened that teachers were deficient in this respect—that they failed to bring forth things new and old. In the United States, it was found that the interest taken by parents in the Schools, was being felt more and more strongly. In Boston, an effort was being made to establish an asylum for vagrant children; and through that institution, the children were being reached, as they had never been reached before. His Reverence, the Roman Catholic Bishop, too, had taken more alarm at that effort than at any other which had been made. The teacher would go to the children with a bible in one hand, and a loaf of bread in the other, and when he approached the parent in this guise, and took him by the hand, it became easy to pour the word of the living God into his heart. The man thus assailed, would throw off Popery, and would be brought into that liberty, wherewith Christ makes his people free. He trusted these schools would bring about union between all denominations of Christians, and between Americans and Canadians. One word more. An American, at Albany, had declared that it was necessary in Sunday Schools to teach duties as well as doctrines; and he wanted all the children of Canada to be taught *to hate Slavery even unto death.*

Rev. Mr. Chidlaw was rejoiced to find himself once more among those who had been his neighbors in the days of his childhood beyond the deep Atlantic. He had been taught to read the Bible in a Sunday School in North Wales. Had he remained there, the child of a peasant, what an inheritance it would have been to have a Welsh Bible, knowledge to read it, and confidence to believe in it! At ten years of age, his parents had brought him to the United States, and had settled near the Reserve of the Wyandot Indians. There was no preaching there; but he had a pious mother and a Welsh Bible, which his mother, his sister, and himself spent the Sunday in reading, till at sixteen years of age, God blessed the reading of that blessed book and made him find a Saviour. A member of a Welsh Baptist Church soon after said to him: "You must now begin to do something for Christ. In Wales we had Sunday Schools: I wish we had some here. You could teach English and I Welsh." That man lived in one of those aristocratic log huts which had two ends to it, and he said: "You shall have one end and I the other." They made a beginning, and soon after he felt an irresistible conviction that he ought to be a Minister. His mother said she would sell her last cow to give him an education; and at last he set out, walking one hundred and forty miles to the seat of learning, with his luggage in a tow bag which his sister had woven for him. He lived there for thirty-two cents a week. He mentioned all this to show how deeply he was interested in this Sabbath School movement. He had met a few weeks ago in the West, with a number of persons who had never seen a locomotive, and the presence of one of those machines created quite a stir in the place, and said mother Whiting, an old lady with spectacles on her nose, while she attentively regarded it: "Can that thing go?" He said: "Oh! yes, wait till the men come and put water into it and kindle the fire, and it will go fast enough!" Well, the Sabbath School cause was a glorious locomotive which God himself had put on the rails, and which his people were called on to keep going. What was the mission of the Sabbath School? To afford religious instruction, with a view to personal salvation, to all the children in the world. If this were so, no wonder that Canada was waking up. No wonder that the United States were rousing themselves from their slumbers. Let it be remembered, too, that God had provided all the appliances which were needed for this work. Look at the position of this great work. The Sabbath School did not come to the pulpit and demand from it the care of the lambs of the flock; nor did it come to the Christian parent and say, we will cancel your obligation. But with kindly smiles and a great heart of love, it offered to co-operate with other agencies. What, then, were its resources? First, it had an open Bible and the agency of that blessed Spirit which takes of the things of God and shows them to his children. Next the work concerned children. When adults were preached to, the message was often met with a repulsiveness that chilled the heart; and yet, the Church of Christ, too often overlooked its vantage ground. It did not, indeed, make too many sacrifices to reach the adult population; but he might very properly ask whether more ought not to be done for the children? At any rate, the circumstances he had mentioned were two great advantages which were possessed by labourers in this cause. He had been connected for twenty years with the American Sunday School Union, which last year, had sent out three hundred missionaries to scatter books and establish schools in thirty-one different States. They had also organised 2,400 new Sabbath Schools, and he told his friends there present, and that venerable Father Smart, that he wanted to go back to the heart of Ohio, and say that he had seen a second edition of Father Cunningham. They all knew Father Cunningham there. In the West, they tried to go ahead. They sowed the seed in a small parcel, and it came up all over the country. In old Switzerland county there were, at a late celebration, thirteen schools with flying banners, and 1,100 scholars. That was where Father Cunningham lived. He was two miles from the school house; but, he said, he never missed a Sabbath for two years. Were there teachers present who had been at the school every Lord's Day for two years? He had heard of a neighborhood, Dearborn, in Indiana, where they needed a school, because they had too many grog shops. That was an excellent reason. He went to try to establish one, and knocked at one door after the other inquiring for a religious family. In answer to that, he was constantly referred to Father Turner, whom he at last found in a little ten feet log shop, making shoes. He said: "I am glad to see you. I have been for a long time looking for some one to help me to get up a Sunday School. I was converted in one at Bristol." The old man got his horse, and preparations were made for holding a meeting in the centre of the district. To accomplish that, however, they had to make many shifts, and were greatly indebted to one old lady who brought a candle and a large fork. For his life, he could not think to what use the fork was to be put; but when it got dark he found out, for his friend stuck the fork through the candle and thus fastened it to the wall of the log house. After he (Mr. C.) had got through with his remarks, Father Turner followed, and made a very effective speech; but when he had done, another man got up and said he understood the whole thing. His father told him it was got up after the revolutionary war, and he doubted not, that it was now taken hold of by that fellow with the black coat, and the Englishman to take away American liberty. Then he told the people how they might be taken in by the affair. The Yankee pedlars, he said, came along and did nothing but talk, and, yet, they afterwards brought in long bills and compelled payment. Finally, he objected teetotally to Sunday Schools, or anything being taught to children about religion. They did not, he said, let children trade horses till they were twenty-one years of age, and he thought they ought to have no religion till they were of that age. After he had spoken for some time another speaker rose and said, that he knew very little about the matter: but he was sure there must be some good in it, or Squire Burnham would not oppose it so much. There was, at that time, but one christian man in all that district; but he (Mr. C.) had since preached to a large congregation from a pulpit whence he could see another Church through the back window. Squire Burnham's influence had declined, and with it horse racing on Sundays; together with four grog shops out of five which formerly existed. Some winters ago he had visited the Mission School at the Five Points, New York, and on his way he saw a gentleman before him with a bundle in his hand. This gentleman descended a cellar, and quickly returned with two little children. He took out of his bundle some clothing, and having attired them in it, went up into a garret, returned, and did the same thing, until he had thus collected thirteen little children, whom he led to that Sunday School. Persons were sometimes kept from this labour by the sacrifices and efforts which it demanded; but those who engaged in it found themselves wonderfully blessed and encouraged. In 1837, he was prosecuting his mission in Northern Ohio, and passing through a wilderness part of the country, he came to a

B

swamp through which the road was but just laid out. He entered upon his journey with a weary heart, and though at first his horse could leap over the logs lying in the swamp, he at length grew fatigued and had to go round them. He thought he must sleep in the woods, and he was just looking out for a dry place for himself and a spice bush for his horse when he heard a dog bark. The sound animated his horse as well as himself; but as the animal could not get through the bushes, he had to dismount and jump from log to log. At length he got to the house; was received by a woman, whose husband was absent, put up his horse and sat down to supper.

Before he began eating, however, he asked for a blessing to accompany it. The good woman at once came to him, and asked— "what, are you a Methodist preacher?" He replied no; but I am the next thing to it. I am a travelling Presbyterian preacher." "Well," said she, "you must preach."—"My good woman I have come a long way and I have seen no one but yourself. However, if you will get me a congregation I will preach willingly." She went to that part of the log house where in other houses there is a mantle piece and taking down a large horn, she blew it at the door. Her husband presently answered the signal. "Oh," said she "John, here's a preacher and we will have a sermon, " by and by several others came in till seventeen were collected. He felt that, if there ever was a time to preach that was it, and they did not ask whether he was a Methodist or not. After he had done, one of the men came forward, however, and said : "Will you lead a class ?"— " I never did ; but if you want to talk about religion go right at it." "Well" replied the man, some of these people have not got religion and they had ought to get it." He was enabled to make a powerful discourse; two of the men came on their knees and there was a good time talking to them. Such was the encouragement the Sunday School teacher sometimes received. Perhaps there were some present who had not been in a Sunday School for three months. (A voice: three years.) That was bad, for Christ expected all to do their duty. He had once seen in a school at Louisville an old colored man who was so blind that he could see nothing. He asked why he came there. " To show," said the other, " that my heart is in it." He hoped then that many of those of whom he had just spoken would let superintendents and teachers see that their hearts were in the schools. If men and women would but become teachers, though there were no classes for them, classes would soon be formed. Mr. Beecher used to say to students who asked him where they should go to preach—" make places. " Just so, let children be gathered in, they would make classes here and, in glory, fill up the Heavenly garners for evermore. He concluded with an appeal to those present to contribute liberally to the collection, enforcing his exhortation by a story of an old lady who belonged to a Church where a bell had been put up. She did not like the bell at all ; but she gave $10 towards it to please her grand daughter. Next Sunday she went to Church ; heard the bell ; and was delighted with the music—such a

change was produced by having $10 invested in the bell.

Rev. Mr. SHORT (Port Hope) said the motto of Sabbath Schools was go ahead, and the spirit which this motto indicated was not confined to the United States, as was proved by the construction of the Grand Trunk Railway, to whose proprietors and to those of the other railways, whose fares had been reduced in favor of the delegates, much gratitude was due. By that means they had been brought to Kingston —now the Capital City of Sunday Schools, and by the very choice made of it for that purpose pointed out as the most fitting place for the seat of the government of the Province. He went on to express his great satisfaction at the proof afforded by the meeting of that Convention of the possibility of all Christians Meeting on terms of friendship and equality to promote the cause of Christ. He had himself entertained prejudices against such meetings ; but he was happy at having got over them. Some feared that they would lead to what was called sheep-stealing—that was to say that the lambs of some pastors flocks would be taken away from them in consequence of these intercommunions. But he thought no such danger was to be apprehended, and at any rate it was a danger equal from all sides. He illustrated the propriety and harmlessness of these unions of Christians at considerable length by a number of familiar examples.

Rev. Mr. BULLARD (Boston) being called on said he would not venture to detain the meeting another moment on that occasion ; but would speak at more length thereafter if another opportunity offered for doing so.

The proceedings of the evening closed with the doxology, "Praise God, from whom all blessings flow" and the benediction.

THURSDAY, FEBRUARY 12TH.

A prayer meeting under the charge of the Rev. Mr. Keough, of Kingston, was held at 7 a.m.

FOURTH SESSION.

The Convention reassembled in the Methodist Church at 9 o'clock.

Devotional exercises occupied half an hour, after which the minutes of the second Session were read and confirmed.

The NOMINATING COMMITTEE recommended that a Committee to consist of—

REV. R. TORRANCE.   MESSRS. GEO. FENWICK,
MESSRS. B. LYMAN,   "   GEO. HARCOURT,
   "   H. A. NELSON, and   SHERIFF TREADWELL

be appointed to examine and report upon the credentials of delegates.—Adopted.

Mr. A. MACALISTER, Chairman of the COMMITTEE ON STATISTICS, reported that they had made up the returns from 204 schools, being the number received up to the opening of the Convention, and presented a statement thereof, (which is here omitted, it being superseded by the appended summary of all the returns.)

The Committee recommended that Sabbath Schools throughout the Province keep regular records from which they may in future be able to answer questions more fully.

The Report excited much interest, and, on Motion, it was ordered, that the returns which, in consequence of coming in too late, had not been included in it, should be added thereto in the printed reports.

Mr. PATON, (Kingston,) on behalf of the Kingston Young Men's Christian Association, invited the members of the Convention to attend a lecture, to be delivered in the evening, before that body, by the Rev. Mr. Bond, in the City Hall. Subject :—Sabbath Schools; their rise and progress.—Mr. Paton stated that a collection towards the expenses of the Convention, might be taken up on that occasion.—Invitation accepted.

The Convention then resumed the discussion which had been interrupted by the adjournment.

Mr. SHERIFF TREADWELL said he had been engaged in Sunday Schools for thirty three years and had visited many in Canada, the United States, and Europe, and in 1849 had seen one in St. Maurice Street Montreal, where there were Infant and Bible classes, and where he thought the management was the best he had ever seen. He had afterwards visited one in Quebec, also exceedingly well conducted. It was worth remarking that the building where this school was held was the only one in the neighbourhood saved at the great fire at Quebec, and that it was preserved by the exertions of the Sunday School scholars. Mr. Treadwell was here interrupted by cries of question.

A DELEGATE expressed a desire to move a resolution, declaring the expediency of organizing a permanent Canadian Sunday School Alliance, to provide means for establishing Sabbath Schools in every School section throughout the country, for all kinds of children ; the said schools to be free from all sectarian names, sectarian teaching, or sectarian books,

The PRESIDENT ruled that such a motion would be out of order, it being foreign to the subject before the Convention, and as it would require to be referred to the Business Committee.

Mr. DUGGAN, (speaking to the question,) conceived that the number of destitute children was greatly exaggerated. It was a libel to say there were 100,000. In the cities there could not be nearly that number, and in the rural districts there could scarcely be any children of the class contemplated by Robert Raikes, as the objects of his exertions.

Mr. BECKET requested leave to withdraw his resolution for the purpose of substituting another. Leave granted. He then moved the following, which was seconded by Mr. Armstrong (Ottawa.)

"That this Convention, recognizing in the Sabbath School an important means of instructing the lambs of the flock as well as an auxiliary to aid parents in training their children in the fear of God—Resolves, that in connection with each Sabbath School there should be a visiting Committee to canvass given districts, for the purpose of bringing in those who do not attend any Sabbath School ; and that teachers should be earnestly requested to aid the

Committee in the work, and that the scholars themselves should be taught that they can do much to bring in those who are without."

Upon being read by the Secretary, the resolution was carried.

The next question on the Docket, viz :—WHAT OUGHT TO BE THE NECESSARY QUALIFICATIONS OF TEACHERS BEFORE THEIR APPOINTMENT TO SABBATH SCHOOL CLASSES? was then stated by the President.

Rev. Mr. HODGSKIN, (Doon) believed this was a question which must be determined not by precise rules ; but by the circumstances of each case. It was desirable that those who were to lead others to Christ should themselves know him, that they might speak with the mouth out of the fullness of the heart. But if a rule were laid down that none should be employed except those truly converted to God, and members of the Church, either that decision must be often set aside or Sunday Schools must in many cases be closed. His first experience on this subject was at Puslinch where a young man, who had been to a meeting of coloured people called on him, to see what could be done for them, and to ask him to visit them. He went and found that only one of them could read. He asked if they had a bible among them. They said they had only a part of one, and handed to him what instead of part of a bible, turned out to be a piece of the American Episcopal Prayer Book. What was he to do in that case? He could not teach them ; nor get converted men to do so. In the place where he now preached, he at one time could not get converted teachers ; but it was otherwise now, for many had manifested a change of heart. In such cases the thing was to do the best that could be done, as his brother from King who stood nearly alone was obliged to do. Yet something must be said about qualification, and that qualification he should say when practicable, should be consistent membership of a Church of Christ. When parties so qualified could not be obtained let the best available be taken, always remembering that there must be no overt immoral conduct on the part of those employed. A delegate present would recollect that on an occasion when he (Mr. H.) had called a meeting to get up a Sunday School, a little girl of fourteen or fifteen years ; but small of her age presented herself for a teacher. He (Mr. H.) thought she was too young, and not possessed of sufficient knowledge. However she got on the list, and kept on though he had tried to keep her off. She proved very efficient. The list of Church members would have shut her out. There were some too, who were not Church members, who might yet be the Lord's hidden ones.

Rev. Mr. MILLER (Ogdensburgh) would not have it presumed on account of what he had said the day before, that he opposed the principle of doing the best you can, when you cannot do what you would like ; but when the qualifications for a Sunday School teacher were asked, he thought the answer should be three-fold— piety, love of the work, and aptness to teach. He remembered the application of an African woman for admission into a Church in Connecticut. They asked her about her evidences of conversion and other questions which she could not answer because she could hardly understand them. They therefore told her, we think perhaps you are scarcely prepared to come to the table. When she heard it, her head fell, and she exclaimed. "Oh I think I love my master." Upon that evidence she was received into the Church. It was good to have men who could show the analogy between the Old and New Testament; who could discourse on the poetry of the psalms, could illustrate bible narrative by eastern customs, and so forth, and persons who did so, by being familiar with the truth theoretically often became practically impressed with it. But love for the work must be the great moving principle everywhere. That was the stimulant of Raikes, of Paxton, and of all who had ever done much for Sunday Schools, and without that there could be no efficient teachers. Again, there must be aptness to teach. He remembered seeing a very learned man, familiar with all the mysteries of pebbles, rocks, trees and plants, and apt to teach all the higher branches of secular knowledge; but placed as a teacher in a common school, at the end of the first year, the examination showed that the class of a comparatively ignorant young man should he placed higher than the one he taught. The learned man shot too high, while the other taught out of the fullness of his own heart, and thus enlisted the sympathies of the children. To all these qualifications add, that which can be obtained through grace only, the influences of the divine spirit on the teacher, and you have a qualified man. None ever went to his class deeply impressed with the worth of souls without having received the blessing of the Spirit's out-pouring—that out-pouring which makes this latter day the day of glory.

Rev. Mr. McDONALD (Fergus) would not wish any man who was not a communicant to be a Sunday School teacher. Yet the circumstances of each case must settle what should be done. He would say to all go and teach; but add as the Scotch minister did; "be sure you know it yourself."

A DELEGATE held that the character of every officer should bear an analogy to his office. Then, what was the office of a Sunday School teacher? To inculcate religious principle, and explain religious emotions. Now, it is true, the anatomist might learn his science by operating on the bodies of others. But he who would know what religious emotion was must learn it from the operations of his own heart. The minister or teacher who did not know the Lord is like a pilot unacquainted with the port towards which he wants to steer. Yet, though desirous of having converted persons for teachers, he would not thrust out others, for this question aroe: What shall we do with *our* children when they grow up? He would not thrust them out because they were unconverted, but keep them in. In his neighborhood, at a recent revival, many teachers and scholars became the subjects of divine grace. Among the teachers was a young lady very amiable and much interested in the school; but unacquainted with the grace of God. But one evening, in retiring from a religious exercise, she said to herself: "this evening the last of my scholars has been converted to God, and shall I remain

unconverted?" She sought the Lord herself, and thus teacher and scholars were all on their way to heaven. One qualification of teachers should be love. A little girl once said: "Pa! you do not pray with me as Ma does." The father, unused to free prayer, read a prayer from a prayer book on his knees by the child. When he had done she addressed him again. "Pa! you did not pray for the dear little girl as Ma does." There was a pathos in the mother's prayer which touched the child's heart. Indeed, the first hint of Sabbath Schools had been given to Raikes by a pious woman who had collected several children and began to talk to them in a class of scripture history, &c.

Rev. Mr. SCOTT (Bath) appealed on this point to the authority of Christ. He chose twelve men to preach His Gospel and one of them was a devil.

A delegate was for setting up a high standard. The practice would always fall low enough.

Mr. NORMAN (King,) thought it would have a very bad effect on the friends of unconverted teachers if they were driven out of the schools.

Mr. TRUESDEL (Sunday School Agent) was often called to places where all was darkness, where, perhaps, there were not more than ten or fifteen families and not one professing Christian among them; yet, with several persons of good moral character, who might be interested in the school cause. Let the agent go among these persons and establish a school, as well as he could, visiting them afterwards and seeing to it, that they were carrying out what was expected of them. He had established many schools in places where there were no professors. He had always called their attention to the importance of having a right qualification. In some of these places the teachers now had their hearts in the work, and followed it with earnestness and Christian principle. In one place, far in the back woods, he had found several persons ready to engage; but he had almost feared to allow them to do so. He did so, notwithstanding, and the time had come for a blessing before his faith had ventured to claim it. He found the hearts of those teachers already giving way before the force of truth. In one place where, in his labor, he had been more perplexed than in any other, for no religious person was to be found there, he met a man who offered to do the best he could, and though for three months after the commencement there was no one to lead the school in prayer, the school could not only be so now, but family altars had been erected in several houses, and five school houses had been built in the woods not far off.

Members of Churches could not themselves go forth to act as agents; but when they could not they should give of their substance to send others forth, and let such agents call all to the work.

God would listen to prayer in behalf of those who had not at present an experimental knowledge of his ways. At Warwick, in Arthabaska county, there was a girl who had had no religious instruction. She desired to go to the school, but as she had no shoes and was approaching womanhood, her mother objected to her attending till she could obtain shoes. At last she said to her mother: "If I ever get to heaven shall I not have to go there barefooted." The argument was irresistible and she went. He often saw that girl afterwards and noticed how the truth was working in her heart. Some time after the school was established he was passing about twelve miles o f, and was invited to the funeral of that girl, who, he found from her parents, had given proof of true piety. She had also brought her father down to his knees, though he had not been used to pray before, and had induced him to erect the family altar, and become, he (Mr. T.) hoped a true Christian.

Messrs. R. Rutherford and J. R. Benson, as mover and seconder, offered a resolution on the subject, several amendments were proposed ; finally, upon motion, the whole were referred to a Committee consisting of—

Mr. R. Rutherford.   Rev. R. Robinson.
Mr. James Stewart.   Mr. Hetherington.

with instructions to draft a resolution, and to report at 3 o'clock.

On motion it was resolved that the last business Session be held to-morrow (Friday) between the hours of half-past 9 A.M., and half-past 12, and that the last hour and a half be left open for voluntary addresses from friends and delegates.

The Rev. F. H. Marling, Chairman of the BUSINESS COMMITTEE, proposed the following votes of thanks, all of which were passed.

To the several committees of arrangements, who with so much labour, thoughtfulness, and care, made such thoroughly efficient provisions for the summoning of the Convention.

To those Railway Companies of Canada ; the Grand Trunk, the Champlain and St. Lawrence ; the Montreal and New York, the Ontario, Simcoe and Huron, the Ottawa and Prescott, the Cobourg and Peterboro ; and the Northern New York Railway Company, who so liberally reduced the travelling fares of delegates from Sabbath Schools, a privilege by which this Provincial Convention has been so much facilitated.

To the conductors of the Press throughout the whole Province, who have aided in announcing, and have advocated the Convention.

To the Local Committee and to the inhabitants of Kingston for the hearty welcome we have received among them, and for the effective arrangements for our meetings, and the generous responses they have made to our large demands on their hospitality.

And to the trustees of the Wesleyan Methodist Church, for the liberality with which they have granted us the use of their beautiful place of worship, in every respect so convenient for our purpose.

It was also voted. That we have had much pleasure in welcoming to this Convention our fellow labourers in the Sabbath School cause from the United States, and thank them for the valuable aid and counsel they have given us.

The question :—" CAN THE GIVING OF REWARDS BE SO CONDUCTED AS TO BE OF ADVANTAGE TO THE SCHOLARS AND TO THE PROSPERITY OF THE SCHOOLS ?" being the fifth on the docket was then introduced.

Rev. Mr. BURPEE (Montreal) believed the subject of rewards was very much misunderstood ; but in the scripture there was ample evidence that reward was held out to every human being, and Christ himself had before him his work and its consequent reward. " Who for the joy that was set before him endured the cross." But many had introduced a sort of reward, differing from the Divine rewards, which were given according to energy and exertion, and the circumstances of each case, and not according to the mere intellectual power of the recipient. In some Sunday Schools those obtained the reward, who made the greatest attainments, and the rest had nothing but the disappointment of defeat. He thought the rewards ought to be equally within the reach of all.

Mr. NORMAN (King) had seen rewards given for learning verses, reciting, &c., but he had never been favorable to it, and at present they never gave anything in his school as a reward, but they gave as a token of love—a course which produced great benefit. He related an occurrence to show the advantage of such presents. A girl was at service in Toronto, and a piece of plate was missing in the house where she lived. On search it was found in her box ; but in the same place there was found a Bible given her by her Sunday School teacher. The girl was friendless, but the discovery of the Bible made her master resolve not to prosecute, and it afterwards turned out that the plate had been stolen by a fellow servant, and placed in her box to divert attention from the real thief. In his school, the teachers gave a little present every new year, but not as a reward. The children were told that they must come to school for the love of Christ.

Mr. HAGAR (Montreal) believed rewards had done much to sustain schools, and cited the account given by Mr. Bullard of the manner in which pupils had been obtained through that means. In Montreal there was a school at the extremity of the city, the Cross, which he lately visited, and promised a bible to every child who would bring another scholar and keep him or her there. In a short time he had to give five or six bibles. But it had happened in Montreal that the order of reward giving had been reversed, for one of the teachers there having invited his class to his house, had been surprised at being presented by the pupils with a very handsome Bible.

Mr. BECKET (Montreal) remarked that there were two kinds of rewards—one sort given for verses learned, recitals, attendance, &c., according to the number of marks or tickets gained by each pupil. He had seen the evil of that from the want of discrimination on the part of teachers, from which it happened that all the children, good and bad, were rewarded alike. The other kind given for bringing scholars to the school he approved of, he thought, however, that no definite action should be taken on this subject for, concerning it, there was great diversity of opinion, and teachers generally would act on their own convictions.

Mr. O'LOUGHLIN (St. James, Kingston) had heard a good deal about the experience of teachers ; but would rather follow the precepts of the bible. He thought the propriety of giving rewards might be amply proved from that book, and then the only question that remained was the best mode of regulating the giving of them. From the beginning to the end of the sacred volume rewards were held out to man. There was the injunction to our first parents, in the day that thou eatest thereof, thou shalt surely die, and going on to Revelations rewards were always held out to man as inducements to serve his master. Jacob served for a reward and got it at last, Caleb and Joshua too were rewarded by enjoying the promised land alone out of all the Israelites who left Egypt. Let the same rule then be followed with children. He had been sixteen years a teacher and twelve years a scholar in a school, presided over by a gentleman now principal of an eminent institution at Birkenhead, the Rev. Jos. Bailey, who always held out rewards to his pupils, and with the best effect. Among them were two shoemakers, one of whom had since been engaged in translating the bible from the Hebrew, and the other was a clergyman in the Church of England. The rewards were given yearly according to the number of tickets held by the pupils for attendance, attention, and lessons.

Rev. Mr. SHORTT (Port Hope) agreed with Mr. Becket that the only question was upon what principle should rewards be given? The ticket system was most troublesome and it happened that under it the worst children got the largest prizes, while modest children who were prevented from coming to school by some cause or other got none at all. With a natural feeling every teacher thought his own class the best, and gave tickets accordingly. It was better to teach the children to regard the Sabbath School as its own reward. Then use might be made of the library by denying books to children to whom it was intended to express disapprobation, the absence of disapprobation being of course approbation. The benefit children derived from the school was reward enough; and if the teachers interested them, they would love to be there.

Mr. HUGHES (Bowmanville) believed rewards were excellent if given in a proper spirit. What would a man in after life take for a reward received at the Sunday School? The rewards he had received had done him a great deal of good, though his teachers were moral only and not pious.

Mr. GEMMILL (Toronto) had found that rewards given in a form that required competition were very injurious. The little ones struggled with all their energies to obtain the prizes, and the object of bringing them to the Saviour was lost sight of in the competition, which was as keen as that carried on by men arrived at maturity. Then, boys, no matter how vicious, might carry off these prizes, while others, patient and industrious, lost them. All the bad passions of the human heart were thus introduced. Instead of rewards thus given, it should be kept in view of the children that the Sabbath School was its own reward. Teachers might, however, properly show their love and sympathy by giving presents as a bond of union between them and the children.

Mr. MATHEWSON (Port Hope) approved of prizes, having always found that the best scholars always carried them off; and then, those who thus learned most scripture and were most attentive were, by the blessing of God, most frequently converted. He had asked children,

whom he had missed from the school,—why they went away? and the reply was,—that they got no books nor tickets. It was necessary, then, to give these things in order to get children, and if they got children to the school, they did them good. This could not be, if the means of drawing children were neglected. He once asked a boy, why he had left the school, saying that they had given him books. "Oh, yes," he replied, "but I get better ones elsewhere, and you give me none when I come late, and I can not come early." He told the boy they would give him rewards; and he came back, and was afterwards a very consistent teacher. Another boy said he would come, if he (Mr M.) would talk about something he could understand. He (Mr. M.) promised to try; and the boy has since been a constant attendant.

Rev. Mr. JEFFERS (Montreal) did not approve in general of giving rewards, nor did he think the bringing of children to the school was a speciality which deserved to be an exception. Children should try to bring in scholars for love, and should not go round electioneering for the sake of getting a bible. It had been said, that God promised to reward man for serving him; but a distinction should be made. He offered spiritual and everlasting rewards certainly—temporal rewards only as they might subserve spiritual interests. That should be the rule in the Sunday School. There were often very bad children, who yet excelled in some speciality, and these children ought not to get rewards, which ought to be given at the end of the year, for general good conduct—the children not being allowed to know beforehand who was to get them.

A DELEGATE thought mischief had arisen from giving prizes, and in his school they found the money once applied to buying them was better disposed of in getting a good library supplied with such modern books as were suitable for Sunday Schools. He would not try to regulate every school by one line, and thought the Convention should avoid going into particulars.

Mr. BROAD (Brantford) believed the question would be best left to teachers and superintendents. He had given in his class rewards for those who could repeat the most verses in the Bible. That had a bad effect; for so many verses were thus gone through that the teacher had no opportunity to comment on them.

Mr. ROGERS (Bowmanville) also thought the subject had better be left open. After the Convention should have decided, every one would go home and act on his own responsibility in his own school. He had found that prizes for the numbers of verses committed to memory, induced some scholars to learn a great many, while the children who had bad memories gave up altogether. Then, when those with good memories had done their best, and could get no higher, they gave up too. The consequence was, that in his school they could get no children to learn verses. Like men with some kinds of appetite, the children with good memories always wanted larger and larger doses to satisfy them.

Several resolutions were brought forward, but it was resolved to lay them all on the table.

On motion it was resolved, that in future the time allowed for each speaker be five minutes, instead of ten.

After prayer the Convention adjourned till 2 o'clock.

FIFTH SESSION.

The PRESIDENT took his seat at 2 o'clock, and half an hour was occupied with devotional exercises.

The minutes of the preceding Session were read and confirmed.

The COMMITTEE ON FINANCE AND PUBLICATION reported the following recommendations which were approved :—

1st. That all Delegates send in their own name, the name of their respective schools, and of their Post Office town, with the number of the printed copies of the proceedings they are prepared to take. Parties ordering to be held responsible for the charge for the same.

2nd. The expense of this Convention being, as nearly as can be made up, about £50, that to meet the same, Delegates assess themselves to the amount of 2s. 6d. each, it being understood that parties may give more if they see fit; and that, if there shall be a greater sum raised than is required, the balance be paid to the Canada Sunday School Union.

The BUSINESS COMMITTEE recommended that the 1st, 2nd, 6th and 10th subject on the printed list, in the circular calling the Convention, be the 6th, 7th, 8th and 9th, for discussion ; the recommendation was approved. The subjects being—

Are any other than strictly religious books suitable for Sabbath School Libraries ?

Infant and Bible classes, their importance and management :

Missionary and kindred objects, how may children be interested in them ?

Conventions general and local, their utility :

The first of these, viz :—

ARE ANY OTHER THAN STRICTLY RELIGIOUS BOOKS SUITABLE FOR SUNDAY SCHOOL LIBRARIES ? was then taken up.

Rev. Mr. HODGSKIN (Doon) thought much depended on the precise meaning of the words of the question. It might well be doubted, if there were not scientific works treating their subjects in a religious point of view, and showing the power and goodness of God, which would be suitable for Sunday School libraries. Yet, he should hesitate to admit them to such libraries in this country, where the excellent arrangements of the government created libraries in connection with the Common Schools, and thus removed any necessity in the Sunday School libraries for books, very proper to be found in them in countries not possessing the literary appliances which distinguished Canada. Whatever the character of the books, they would be given out on the Sabbath, and if he had not misapprehended the question, it might be better stated in this way :—" Are any books, not adapted for Sabbath reading, adapted for Sunday School Libraries ?" His idea was that they were not. He therefore moved, seconded by Mr. Becket of Montreal—

" That it is the opinion of this Convention that those books only which are suitable for Sabbath reading are suitable for Sabbath School libraries."

Mr. FRASER (Goderich) apprehended that books which taught Christ were those alone fitted for Sunday School Libraries, and those which treated most of His person and work were, therefore, the most suitable. Mere scientific books, though they treated of the power and wisdom of God, ought to be given out only in very rare cases. He would prefer works which treated of Christ doctrinally.

Mr. RUTHERFORD (Peterboro) remarked that, if the question were decided in the manner recommended by Mr. Hodgskin the question would still arise what is fit for Sabbath reading. He thought the answer to the inquiry before the Convention would depend very much on the character of the mind of the person to whom the books were to be given. There was a book called "Fern Leaves for Fanny's Little Friends." Was such a book fit for the School Library or not ? It was of a high moral character and in his opinion might be suitable. Dry theological works fit for converted persons might be quite unsuitable for children the majority of whom were unconverted. He would give to such children the thing nearest to that which he would desire them to read.

Rev. Mr. HODGSKIN (Doon) did not wish to enter into the question of what books were fit ; but only to lay down a principle, leaving the application to every man's conscience.

Mr. S. B. SCOTT (Montreal) read an extract from the report of a Sabbath School teachers Convention in Massachusetts to this effect.

" They have examined the catalogues of eighteen schools represented in this Convention, containing in all a fraction over 10,000 volumes. Of these, about 2,100 volumes, or a little more than one-fifth of the whole, were considered by the Committee as " not religious." Leaving out nine schools, the catalogues of the remaining nine, containing 6,880 volumes, of which 1,950, or 28¼ per cent., are " not religious." Taking three schools only, and we have 1,525 volumes, of which 625, or more than 40 per cent., are " not religious."

It will be proper here for the Committee to " define their position." The term religious, they suppose to comprehend the following general classes of books :—

1st. Books that corroborate the truths of the Bible, or illustrate its meaning, as for example, Layard's Nineveh, or Hackett's Illustrations of Scripture.

2nd. Such as explain the doctrines of the Bible, or enforce its precepts, such as Truth Made Simple, by Todd ; The Corner Stone, by Abbott ; and several of the works by " Charlotte Elizabeth. "

3rd. Such as are fitted to develope personal piety, to prepare the reader for the service of God on earth, and the enjoyment of his presence in heaven ; for instance, Pilgrim's Progress, Hugh Fisher, Eagle Hill, The Wilmot Family, Willie Grant, and Green Hollow, by Dr. Ide.

As not included under either of these three divisions, the Committee felt constrained to reject a considerable number of books which they found in one or more of the libraries they examined, and which may be classified as follows :—

1st. *Secular National Histories*, such as Goldsmith's History of Greece, and Macaulay's History of England.*

2nd. *Historical Memoirs and Narratives*, not pervaded by a religious spirit,—such as the entire interesting series recently prepared by Abbott, and the historical narratives of Banvard.

3rd. *Personal Memoirs of Statesmen and Military Heroes* not written with a religious purpose,—as the Lives of Bonaparte, Lafayette, Jackson, Taylor, the Life of Webster, by Banvard, or his Private Life and Correspondence, by Lanman.

4th. *Books of Travel and Personal Adventure*, not confirming the truth or illustrating the meaning of Scripture,—as, The Captive in Patagonia, Roughing it in the Bush, Adventures in the Gold Regions, Rollo on the Rhine, in Paris, Switzerland, &c.

5th. *Works of Fiction*, the reading of which is not fitted to make a religious impression on the mind,—books, in which religious truth is not so closely interwoven with the narrative, that the reader is compelled to take both or none. To this class belong the largest proportion of books, not religious, to be found in our Sabbath School Libraries. We may mention, under this head, Aunt Mary's Library Series, Swiss Family Robinson, Abbott's Rollo and Lucy, Grace Aguilar's Works, all or nearly all the host of books written by T. S. Arthur, the Paul Creyton Series, — (Father Brighthopes, Hearts and Faces, &c.,) — Mrs. Tuthill's books,—(Onward, Queer Bonnets, &c.,) —Influence, or Evil Genius, Two Lives, The Lamplighter, Ida May, &c.

6th. *Miscellaneous Books*, under which we specify Lotus Eating, and Chamber's Miscellanies, and Papers for the People, and Parley's Cabinet Library, these serials making some forty volumes in all.

In regard to books of an absolutely "injurious tendency," the Committee are happy to say that their number is small, as compared with the whole number of books in the libraries. They are numerous enough, however, to call for immediate scrutiny on the part of those whose duty it is to have this matter in charge. We would invite such to inquire into the *religious* influence of such books as Ruth Hall, Fashion and Famine, Life and its Aims, Carlyle's Essay's, Easy Nat, Gustavus Lindorm, Autobiography of an Actress, The Wonderful Mirror, &c., &c.

In view of the whole subject, and after mature deliberation, the Committee express it as their solemn conviction that the Sabbath School Library should be held sacred to books of a decidedly religious character.

If it be deemed desirable to furnish secular books to the members of our Sabbath Schools, let such books be kept in a separate library and distributed on a week-day and not on the Sabbath. This plan has already been successfully

---

* Every book named in this report was found in one or more of the libraries examined by the Committee.

adopted in some schools, and will soon be introduced into others.

In closing their report, the Committee suggest the necessity of greater care in the selection of libraries. This matter, it is feared, has been too often done at hap-hazard. It should be made a subject of prayer,—of careful, thoughtful attention. The duty should be devolved on a competent Committee appointed by the school, or, better still, by the church ; said Committee to make full report of their doings. This would tend to check the temptation which irresponsible persons might feel to purchase an unsuitable book for the library, that they might have the reading of it gratis. It should be considered unwise, also, to leave the selection, as is sometimes done, to publishers or booksellers. The responsibilities connected with this subject are too vast and momentous to justify a careless, negligent or selfish discharge of the duties it involves. May God grant to his servants, in this thing, the spirit of wisdom, fidelity, and sound discretion.

Mr. MATHEWSON (Montreal) objected to any other than strictly religious books for Sunday School Libraries. All the books admitted into such libraries were endorsed by the school teacher, and were taken home to be read on Sunday. The Sunday School paper was open to the same objection. It contained many things altogether unfit for Sunday reading. There were plenty of secular and moral papers ; could not religion then be made sufficiently interesting to fill one paper with reading matter fit for Sunday ?

Mr. CAMPBELL (Carleton Place) agreed with the previous speaker. He himself had been converted by the reading of a library book.

Mr. FOSTER (Smiths Falls) held that the teaching in the schools ought to be enforced by the books sent out from the library. In his school there was not a single book of an objectionable character. They were all religious biographical sketches, short sermons, or scriptural histories. The Common School Libraries, Mechanics' Institutes, &c., furnished plenty of general reading and the Sunday School Libraries ought to be composed of strictly religious books.

Rev. Mr. McDONALD (Fergus) thought the best advice a parent could give to a child leaving home was : "keep the Sabbath Holy." Every individual who did so would be holy. The intention of the Sunday School teacher therefore should be to give none but religious books out on Sundays. There was much looseness of practice on this head, and the minister was frequently pained to see even what was called the religious newspaper make its appearance on the Sunday, because of the mixed character of its contents. Even Sunday School papers, such as the Penny Gazette and others of that class were not fit for the Sunday.

Rev. Mr. DENISON (Albany) believed their was no fear of the books becoming too religious. The only fear was of their not being religious enough, and of thus letting down the high standard set up in the Bible. It was too much the custom to teach children that if they were respectful to their parents, and teachers, and if they did their duty to society when they grew up that was all that was required. This should be guarded against, and as to the book which had been mentioned, (Fern leaves) he felt it his duty to say that there was not a really Christian Sabbath School in the United States, which would admit it to its library. There was no objection to such books elsewhere ; but ministers, teachers, and superintendents were as the representatives of Jesus Christ, guardians of the school, which was the nursery of the Church. Now if the nursery were filled with a miasma, the children would grow up the children of the Devil rather than of God. It must be remembered that books from the School library, went out with a sort of blessing of the pastor and teachers. Was it fit then that they should contain one grain of wheat and perhaps a bushel of chaff ? No—

" Christ and his cross are all our theme,
" The mysteries that we speak.

Dr. Main (Kingston) believed there had been too much laxity in this point of practice, and did not exempt himself from the censure, others might feel that some blame attached to them, for not having examined with sufficient strictness the books which appeared on the library shelves. The teachers were responsible that such books should be unimpeachable—that was to say strictly religious. There is a wide difference between such books and those containing one grain of wheat and a bushel of chaff. If any means could be found of selecting books, to which the convention could give its *imprimatur* it would be doing good not only to Canada, but perhaps also to the United States, England, Europe, and the world. Nor was that impracticable, for it must be a poor religion if its professors could not say what books were truly religious.

Mr. Oliver (Paris) conceived that though in other countries, scientific books perhaps might be properly admitted to Sunday School libraries, there could be no reason for doing so in Canada, where general reading was so amply provided for. He recommended teachers, on seeing their own libraries supplied, to turn all their attention to the carrying out of the law. Then society would be supplied with literary and scientific works, and Sabbath School libraries with the description of literature which might be looked for in them.

Mr. D. Rose had experienced the difficulty of being obliged to undertake the illustration of Scripture without having access to books of travel written by religious men ; and since he had had such books in his own library, he had found that those who did not possess them, were unable to explain passages of Scripture as fully as was necessary. It was well, therefore, to have such books in Sunday School libraries. It might be said, they could be had in the Common School libraries. But unfortunately, he was situated in a locality, where so far the people had not availed themselves of the law in any one School section of the township. He thought there were works on science which ought never to be excluded from Sunday School libraries ; for instance, the works of Dick and Hugh Miller, the latter on that very science which had been made the instrument of spreading infidelity in the land.

Rev. Mr. Marling (Toronto) knew a Sunday School where the managers had taken the trouble to order a number of books on speculation, every one of which they caused to be read over by members of a committee, appointed for that purpose, who reported on the character of the

book. Not till every book had been thus inspected, was it allowed to go into the library of the school. One plan of procuring libraries, was to purchase from some publishing society one or two hundred books ; but the inconvenience of this plan was, that new books were not procured in that way, as they were copyright, and the societies could not, therefore, get hold of them. He thought persons who got up School libraries ought to go over the booksellers' catalogues themselves, especially the catalogues of such houses as Carter and Nesbit.

Rev. Mr. Jeffers desired to place on the record a condemnation of all books of fiction. The mere idea that they were not true prevented them from having a good effect ; and the reading of religious fictions led to the reading of other fictitious works. Religious fictions had the great evil of all romances—they brought together surprizing events in a manner which did not occur in life, and they by this means created a state of hope and expectation which was highly injurious. Besides they always brought their heroes to a successful termination of their difficulties and thus led children not to make up their minds to those sacrifices which are necessary on the part of those who desire to serve God.

Mr. Foote (Buffalo) with reference to what Mr. Marling had said on the subject of selection, related that on one occasion he had gone into a book store in connection with which a depot of religious books was kept, and had seen the astonishing recklessness with which selections were sometimes made. He had seen a man purchase eighty-five volumes, taking perhaps ten minutes for examination. By and by, the friends of this gentleman found something erroneous in one of the works, and on closer inspection, twenty-one of them were found to contain teaching opposed to the Bible. He thought it was better to go to a Society which afforded some guarantee, rather than make so superficial an examination. There were booksellers who sold thousands of books as Sunday School Books, who had no religious principles at all.

Mr. D. McKay (Montreal) approved of what the Rev. Mr. Jeffers said, and thought many of the " religious works of fiction" were more highly coloured than some of the novels of the present day. The heroes of such works were represented as possessing hearts very different from what the Bible taught, and in order to counteract much of the *light reading* (often very licentious) that was so common in our day, works of History and Christian Travellers, and even scientific works, such as geology and Astronomy, were worthy of being admitted into a Sunday School library, for they directed the pupil "from nature up to nature's God." The assertion that the cause of Christianity might suffer from the investigation of scientific men, was a libel ; as such labors went to confirm, not to upset the truths of revelation.

Mr. Hagan (Montreal) remarked that in his school they had a Committee to examine books, and that it was the fault of Sunday School managers, not of publishers, who made books to sell, if bad books got into the libraries.

The Rev. Mr. Hodgskin's resolution was then re-read.

Whereupon it was moved in amendment by the Rev. Mr. Jeffers, seconded by Mr. J.

Taylor, and resolved :—That this Convention conceives it to be of great importance that the books in our Sabbath School libraries be of a strictly religious character, and particularly that books of a merely scientific or literary interest, and that books of religious fiction be excluded as tending to produce effects not in accordance with the specific object of Sunday School instruction.

The Committee appointed to prepare a resolution on the question,—WHAT OUGHT TO BE THE NECESSARY QUALIFICATIONS OF TEACHERS BEFORE THEIR APPOINTMENT TO SABBATH SCHOOL CLASSES? presented two resolutions, one from the majority and one from the minority of the Committee,— upon both being read the question stood first on the resolution of the minority, viz :—

Resolved,—That the requisite qualifications of a thorough Sabbath School teacher are accredited piety, aptness to teach and a love of the work ; but in cases where such teachers cannot be obtained, the best procurable may be employed ; it being always understood and provided that through the superintendent or others the children of every Sabbath School, be brought into contact with the instructions of truly pious persons, to the end that the great object of Sabbath School instruction, the glory of God and the salvation of souls may be secured.

To which it was moved in amendment by the Rev. Mr. Marling seconded by Rev. Mr. Hodgskin, and carried that all after the word "employed," be omitted. The resolution as amended was then put and carried, after which the resolution of the majority, viz :—"That this Convention records its convictions that only pious persons are properly qualified, to be teachers in Sabbath Schools, and none but members of Evangelical Churches and persons of high moral character, should be placed in so responsible a position," was rejected.

The Convention proceeded to consider, the seventh subject on the docket, viz :—"INFANT AND BIBLE CLASSES, THEIR IMPORTANCE AND MANAGEMENT."

Rev. Mr. HODGSKIN believed that the great error parents made was not beginning with their children soon enough. They seemed to think that there must be a certain length of time before children should be taught the knowledge of God. Dr. Beattie had had an idea that his son should be taught nothing of the Supreme Being till he was six years of age, and then the doctor sowed some seed in the form of his son's initials. When the son saw it come up, he at once referred to his father as having sowed the seed. His father put off the question for some time ; but at length acknowledging himself as the author of the fact, thence took occasion to direct the attention of the boy to the author of all things. That was a wise act ; but considering the uncertainty of life and the certainty of death it would have been more wise and more loving to have taken an earlier period t˚ show that there was a God to be loved and served. Perhaps however, some were deterred by the difficulty of speaking on these subjects to a child. He knew that when the Rev. Mr. Jay was asked to address the children at Rowland Hill's church, he had replied that he never could address children. It was not every minister who would make a good Sabbath School teacher ; nor every teacher who would make a teacher of infant classes. It required some one who did not think the work unimportant, and who would be able to give the little crumbs of the word to the young children.

Mr. HARCOURT (Toronto) had given instruction for a long time in an Infant school. Some time ago, a person came to him, and said she remembered the manner in which he (Mr. H.) had illustrated the account of the raising of the Syrophœnician woman, and that that illustration had taught her more than anything else the best mode of explaining the scriptures. Teachers who were fit for their business, went among the little ones with infantile ideas, and elucidated the histories and doctrines of the bible by illustrations drawn from domestic life ; so that, if the children are even unable to understand at the time, they treasure it up in their memories, and comprehend it later in life. An infant school teacher should neither be too young nor too old ; but one who had vivacity and cheerfulness, who could, if need were, sing with the children. He remembered a teacher speaking to children thus : " What is prayer ? " One said : " It is talking with God." " Nothing else ? When you go home to your mother and ask for bread and butter, is that nothing but talking to your mother ? You feel the need of what you ask for, do you not ? " " Yes." " Well, that is prayer ; it is asking God for what you want." These were the kind of illustrations fitted for the young. He believed that the want of bible classes might be largely supplied by Infant schools.

Mr. PEARSON (Toronto) knew of two cases of conversion by the instrumentality of the Infant class, in the school to which he belonged ; one was a little girl, seven years of age, converted by means of pictures, which were used in the school, and which taught her to apprehend the truths of the gospel. She died, and her last words were words of comfort—that she was going to heaven. Through her expressions, a child of four years old, was also converted. He did not think a child must be twelve or thirteen years of age before it could apprehend the gospel. He had known many of seven years old converted to God. In his school, the teacher did not keep the children long in one position ; but got them to stand up after sitting some time, made them frequently clap their hands, sing, and so forth. They were almost all under eight and some under six years of age. The school was in Richmond street, Toronto.

Mr. B. LYMAN (Montreal) mentioned that at the first Sunday School where he attended forty years ago, there were but seven children, and the oldest was but eight years of age. His venerable friend, Mr. Smart, was the means of establishing that infant class. He (Mr. L.) was seven years old then and had continued a scholar up to the present time. True he had become a teacher, but he had been learning all the time. He superintended the school of the Church to which he belonged in Montreal, but had visited many others. He could bear witness to the excellence of the school last mentioned, also to that of Dr. Tyng's school, New York, conducted on similar principles. At one time the teacher of the infant school with which he was connected taught the A B C, but he broke that up and got the children placed under a person who could sing and interest them. Pictures, too, illustrative of scripture history, were placed in prominent positions in the school room, and the children were catechised upon such portions of the bible as the parable of the prodigal. The narrative was explained, and from it they were taught that all must go to Christ. At seven or eight years of age when the children could read the bible, they were taken to form other departmental classes, and from the adult classes which followed these, teachers, thus trained up in the school, were selected. The teachers and the children, therefore, grew up together. As to teachers for infant classes it had been well said they should neither be too young nor too old. He had taken a young lady and taught her to instruct the classes, and now it was a punishment for the children to be kept away.

Rev. Mr. Chidlaw had long tried to find in any prison a Sunday School graduate, and he had not found one yet, and never expected that he should. He was, therefore, glad to see that Canada had the whole system, infant, ordinary, and adult classes. He repeated that he had never in his experience of the criminal classes found an offender who had passed through the infant, the ordinary, and the adult classes. One might as well seek an Angel in the realms of darkness as expect to meet with such a child abandoning the works of light and love and becoming a convict within the fangs of the law. It was, nevertheless, true, that in general Christians did not begin soon enough with the child. Let the teachers, then, go home and think for the little ones. God would honor them in their work, and permit the truths of christianity, adapted to the capacity of the young, to be by their lips and examples impressed upon the tender, confiding, and impressible minds of the children. The scholars were often lost to the Sunday School class because their affections were not enchained early enough. But set a young man or young woman, a matron or father, in a circle of twenty, or thirty children, there was no difficulty about retaining their attention. The child would grow up and be transferred to the second grade, and there he must be held on to, and not allowed to slip away till he was passed to the adult class. Last Sunday, in Cincinnatti, he went to the rooms of the Young Men's Christian Association, and saw there one hundred and forty young men, each with a bible in his hand. There was hope for a country where the young men were interested in such a study.

Rev. Mr. Bullard believed there was no age from the mothers lap to the grave unsuited to Sabbath Schools. In Massachusetts and elsewhere in the United States, the plan was to have infant classes of one hundred to one hundred and fifty. But they had also succeeded in interesting older persons. A minister told him that if a member of his Church did not belong to the Sabbath School, he should feel it his duty to go and converse with him, as he would do if the man were neglecting family prayer. He could see no good reason why an adult should not go to Sabbath School, which could not be equally well urged by the children for staying away. As to common schools, of course they understood that adults had finished that part of their education; but was there any time when a man could be said to have finished his education in the Bible? Was there any reason why if a man did not go in as a teacher he should not go as a pupil? It was one thing to read the Bible and another to study it. He appealed to many who were accustomed to read one or more chapters daily, whether they did not sometimes, if they missed their mark, find themselves doubting whether they were not reading the same chapter which they had perused the day before? But did any who had studied a chapter at school ever forget having read it? And this social manner of study prepared the mind to listen with more interest to the things of God. What advantages a political speaker had over a preacher? How far more fixed the attention which the former attracted, and why? Because every man present had been prepared by reading the newspapers, for the discussion of the speaker's subject. The speaker concluded by mentioning that the Chicopee School contributed $10 a month to the Sabbath School mission, and when he went there to preach, the minister told him he must take up a collection. He said no, that would be too much. "Oh yes," was the reply, "it wont hurt them." After he (Mr. Bullard) had addressed the people, he told them he was going, as their minister had said he must, to take up a collection, but instead of the usual appeal made on such occasions he would tell them he thought they gave as much as they ought. They gave him $52 more.

In answer to questions, he stated that he thought it desirable that adult or Bible classes should meet in the same room, in which the ordinary classes meet, and at the same hour. In the States they usually had the gentlemen in one room and the ladies in another. They took turns to become monitors, and the pastor sometimes had a class of ladies and gentlemen himself. Also, that adults rarely learned scripture except for the lessons.

Mr. Thompson (Rochester) had seen children of 2½ years of age in the schools of the United States. Then, when they were eight or nine years of age, they were told: "If you bring in six or eight scholars, a class of six or eight of you may graduate." Thus, the school was kept full. The scholars passed through from the Infant school till they became teachers. The Bible classes should be where the superintendent could see them. He had known lawyers come and take away the best scholars to form Bible classes. Then they did not come, and their absence for two Sundays sufficed to drive away the scholars. Nineteen years ago, he put his foot down against that. The Bible class, now the most interesting in the school, would not go away; but if they were taken into a second room, they would quickly fall off.

Mr. Denison found the influence of Bible classes so great, his congregation had had doubts if they should not do away with a service, in order that all the congregation might attend the Bible class. If they could get them established, slavery would soon cease to exist in America. Bible classes taught the great practical duties of life, and would reform the world.

The Rev. R. Torrance moved, seconded by Mr. J. A. Sexsmith, and it was resolved,—

That this Convention feels deeply the importance of Infant and Bible classes in connection with Sabbath Schools, and earnestly recommends their establishment throughout the Province; and recommends with regard to their management.

1st, That Bible classes be held in the room with the other classes, unless special reasons exist for the contrary.

2nd, That Bible classes be under the teaching of the minister of the congregation, or of some other person well instructed in the contents of the Holy Scriptures and apt to teach.

3rd, That it be the constant effort in the Bible class to qualify for entering into fellowship with the Christian Church.

4th, That infant classes be not held in the same room or not at the same hour as the other classes.

5th, That for infant classes particular attention be paid to select teachers of known piety and who will enter into the feelings of the children, and who know how to engage their attention, or to hearken to suggestions on this point

The Committee on Finance and Publications recommended that the publication of the proceedings of the Convention be confided to a special Committee, with full power to adopt whatever steps they might think necessary, and the nominating Committee having suggested—

Messrs. H. A. Nelson, Montreal.
  "   S. B. Scott,   "
  "   J. A. Mathewson,   "
  "   J. W. Taylor,   " and
  "   James Stewart, Kingston.

It was moved by Mr. D. Beadle, seconded by Mr. Goodfellow, and resolved,—

That that Committee be composed of the Delegates named.

The President then submitted the eighth topic, viz :

MISSIONARY AND KINDRED OBJECTS—HOW MAY CHILDREN BE INTERESTED IN THEM ?

Mr. Thompson (Rochester) had begun this work many years before, by getting penny subscriptions to educate children in India. He recollected a missionary who once had charge of the school coming and telling the children :— " Your contributions towards education enabled me to leave my post, and was the occasion of Mr. Thompson taking my place." The idea of having effected something, worked like electricity. The school children began again, and contributed for educating five more. Their contributions were always increasing. They gave $205 in one Sunday. A generation was in course of training which, by and bye, would exercise a mighty influence ; and he believed that here the Finance Committee might go among the children and get money to pay all expenses. Let them be taught to spend for the Lord, otherwise, the money would be spent in worse ways.

Mr. Baylis (Montreal) thought more was required than to teach the mere giving of money. They should be encouraged to decide as to the objects on which the money should be spent in order that they might be interested in the work of missions, and learn to take part in public business connected with religious societies.

The Rev. Mr. Hodgskin moved, seconded by the Rev. Mr. Elliot :—

That this Convention earnestly recommends, that wherever practicable there be, beyond the taking up of periodical contributions, the organization in Sabbath Schools of Juvenile Missionary Societies, such societies holding meetings at stated brief intervals for the purpose of giving and receiving missionary intelligence and for the transaction of business.

Rev. Mr. Short rose to move in amendment that the words " and temperance" be inserted in the resolution, after the word " missionary."

Rev. Mr. Hodgskin, however, called Mr. Short to order, as the subject of total abstinence formed no part of the programme of proceedings which were understood to be the object of assembling the Convention, and particularly as it was foreign to the subject of the resolution.

The President ruled that the amendment was not in order.

Rev. Mr. Bulland in answer to the question, how to interest children in missions? would say, that the way was to get them into operations they could understand. They could understand for instance what missionaries were doing to gather children in their own land, and it would be well to let them receive letters direct from the missionaries so employed. He often felt stimulated and encouraged by the necessity of thus reporting to Sabbath Schools. Let young and tender sensibilities be touched by compassion for the young, and the children would soon come up to the work of Sunday School extension. Last year his Society had issued a circular, stating that every school which would give $50 would receive a letter direct from a missionary. Fifty or one hundred schools sent in immediately from $50 to $100 each. Children who contributed 50 cents had a beautifully engraved certificate with a pictorial receipt at the back.

It was then moved in amendment to the resolution before the Convention by Rev. Mr. Marling, seconded by Mr. Ainslie, that in the opinion of this Convention it is a most important element in the christian training of the young to make them take an active part in sustaining the great benevolent movements of the day, and that it therefore recommends that the officers of Sabbath Schools make arrangements for the regular communication of missionary intelligence to the scholars and the receiving of their contributions.

And the amendment being put to the meeting was carried.

The Committee on Finance reported the following statement :—

Amount due J. C. Becket, Montreal, for printing circulars,...........£25	8	9
Travelling expenses of invited Delegate 3	18	9
Gas for Public Meeting at City Hall...................... 1	10	0
Local expenses, printing, Sexton, stationery, &c................ 7	15	3
Due J. W. Taylor, Montreal, for postages, telegraphs, &c., paid by him, (estimate) 8	10	0
	£47	2	9

CONTRA.

Collection at Public
Meeting............£19   5   5½
Assessment of Dele-
gates............ 23   5   9
      ————— 42 11 2½

Deficiency...... £4 11 6½

On motion it was resolved to take up a collection to meet the deficiency.

MAYOR AND CITIZENS OF KINGSTON.

It having been stated, that, owing to the pre-
valence of scarlet fever in the city, and the un-
expected large number of Delegates present, all
the Delegates are not enjoying the hospitalities
of the people of Kingston; about seventy-five of
them having had to go to hotels, some conversation arose on the propriety of dividing the
expense. Whereon, the Treasurer of the city of
Kingston rose and stated that he was authorised
by the Mayor to say, that he and the citizens of
Kingston (not the Corporation) would see that
all hotel expenses were paid.

It was immediately resolved, that the thanks
of this Convention are tendered to the Mayor
and citizens of Kingston for their extremely
handsome hospitality.

Thanks were also voted to the Members of
the Kingston Young Men's Christian Association, for the warm consideration they had
shown for the interests of the Convention.

Thanks were due to the proprietor of Iron's
Hotel, for liberally entertaining delegates at
one half of his customary charge.

It was announced that the Rev. Mr. Bullard,
Rev. Mr. Elliot, and the Rev. Mr. Childlaw
would address the meeting in the City Hall,
after the Rev. Mr. Bond had finished his lecture.

After devotional exercises the Convention
adjourned till 9 a.m., on Friday morning, with
the view of enabling delegates to be present at
the lecture in the City Hall.

FRIDAY, FEBRUARY 13.

A prayer meeting was held this morning at
7 A.M.

SIXTH SESSION.

The Convention met at 9 o'clock, pursuant
to adjournment, and, after half an hour of devotional exercises, the minutes of the preceding
Session were read and confirmed.

The minutes of the former Sessions were also
re-read.

The FINANCE COMMITTEE presented a final
report, as follows:—

Amount previously reported...... £42 11 2½
Amount of Collection.......... 6 15 5½
      —————
      £49 6 8

CONTRA.

Amount as per former Report 47 2 9

     Balance........ £2 3 11
To be paid to the Canada Sunday School
Union.

2nd. Amount handed to the Committee for reports of proceedings with
orders for as many copies as the sum
will pay for.....................£20 19 3

3rd. Seventy names were handed to the
Committee with orders for 1,000 copies of the
report at such a price as they can be afforded.

4th. The Committee have to allude to the
unbounded generosity of the Mayor and citizens
of Kingston, for the handsome manner in which
Delegates have been entertained during their
sojourn in Kingston. Not being satisfied with
filling their dwellings to overflowing, they pay
the bills of those who were under the necessity
of going to hotels.

The Report was received and adopted.

The ninth and last subject was then pro-
pounded for discussion:—

"CONVENTIONS, LOCAL AND GENERAL—THEIR
UTILITY."

The Rev. Mr. HODGSKIN thereupon moved, seconded by Mr. MORE, of Quebec:

1st. That we cannot but recognise the great
utility of Sabbath School Teachers' Conventions,
and therefore deem it desirable that arrangements be now made for holding Local or Provincial Assemblies of that character in succeeding years.

2nd. That such Conventions be composed of
Delegates appointed by Sabbath Schools or Sabbath School organizations, holding what are
commonly regarded as evangelical sentiments,
viz.:

1st. The Inspiration of the Scriptures.
2nd. The Deity of Christ, and the Personality
and Deity of the Holy Spirit.
3rd. The total depravity of human nature.
4th. The Vicarious Sacrifice of Christ.
5th. Justification by Faith alone.
6th. Regeneration by the Holy Spirit.
7th. The Eternity of future rewards and pu-
nishments.

Mr. RUTHERFORD, instead of having the resolution in its present shape, would like to stop
with the words "Evangelical sentiments," as he
did not want any platform laid down. All
knew what "evangelical" meant, and perhaps
if they went further, they might get into dis-
cussions on doctrine. He moved, seconded by
Mr. Dobson, that all after the words evangelical sentiments, be struck out.

Two DELEGATES expressed an opinion that the
Convention should keep its standard held aloft.

Rev. Mr. WILSON (Kingston) approved of the
statement of the basis on which the future Conventions were to organize. The term "evangelical," whether in Canada or the United States,
was most indefinite; and it was time to do away
with it. No one would doubt that these
were the principles which should be taught in

Evangelical Sunday Schools; and if any schools did not maintain those principles, they ought not to be countenanced. Was the Convention to countenance Morrisonianism, or the doctrine of the merely subjective work of the Holy Spirit?

Rev. Mr. Hodgskin thought denominational names ought not to be mentioned.

Mr. Bkqo (London) approved of the first part of the resolution—all the more, because his prejudices against Conventions had been removed by what he had seen of the unity and largeness of heart of brethren of different denominations present. As to the latter part, he did not object to the principles laid down; but did not know that it was necessary to lay them down.

The amendment being put was lost. Rev. Mr. Hodgkin's motion was then carried.

Mr. J. W. Taylor (Montreal), seconded by Mr. D. Beadle, moved the following resolutions :—

1st. That it be recommended to hold local Conventions in the following cities, viz. :—

London	in the years	1858	and	1860.
Hamilton	"	1859	"	1861.
Toronto	"	1858	"	1860.
Kingston	"	1859	"	1861.
Ottawa	"	1858	"	1860.
Montreal	"	1859	"	1861.
Quebec	"	1858	"	1860.

And that a Provincial Convention be held in the City of Kingston, in the year 1862.

2nd. That the superintendents of Sabbath Schools in the several cities be appointed committees to prepare for the first local conventions in these respective cities, and that at each of them, committees be appointed to arrange for each succeeding one, and that it be recommended to all these committees to confer with one another for the purpose of preventing the occurrence of two conventions at the same date.

3rd. That at each of the local conventions held in the years 1860 and 1861, except at that held in the City of Kingston, one person be appointed to correspond with the committee hereafter provided for, and to aid it in arranging for the Provincial Convention to be held in the city of Kingston in 1862.

4th. That at the local convention held in the city of Kingston in 1861, a committee be appointed to arrange for the Provincial Convention to be held in that city in the year 1862: the said committee to consult the individuals appointed at the local conventions as provided for in the preceding resolution and with them to determine the date for holding the Provincial Convention and to do whatever else may appear necessary to ensure success.

5th. That the following subjects be recommended for consideration at the local conventions of 1858 and 1859.

1st. Best mode of regulating schools and keeping records.

2nd. The duties of teachers.

3rd. The relation of the school to the Church.

4th. Children who cannot read, shall they be taught to read or taught from the Bible orally?

5th. The claims of communities, without schools and unable to organize them without assistance, upon those which enjoy their advantages.

And that the various committees appointed to prepare for these conventions correspond with each other for the purpose of selecting a number of subjects to be recommended to them for consideration at the respective succeeding local conventions. And that at the Provincial Convention, to be held at Kingston in 1862, a review of the whole be taken, so that a comparison of results may be obtained and the experience of those who have carried out the suggestions made at the local conventions may be related.

6th. That each committee endeavour to secure suitable persons, each to take one of the subjects determined on into consideration in time to enable him to study it carefully, so that it may be brought before the convention in a complete and comprehensive manner.

7th. That all the conventions provided for in the preceding resolutions claim the utmost faithfulness, wisdom and energy of the respective committees.

After a somewhat rambling conversation and several proposals to amend the resolutions which appeared to the Convention to possess too much of a legislative character.

The mover stated that he had no desire whatever to press his resolutions upon the Convention. He brought them forward merely as recommendations, which would be carried out or not, just as future circumstances may dictate; but he felt that it was important to place respon ibility somewhere; for unless that is done, adverse circumstances and difficulties are permitted to exercise greater influence than they otherwise would. Moral responsibility, by being a powerful motive to action, generally counteracts opposing influences, and leaves the way clear for action, when reason points to its expediency. He felt that for local Conventions, it was especially necessary to make some provision; responsibility should be felt, and, as far as possible, a system determined on. Of course, the naming of certain places in the resolutions was not intended to preclude other places from getting up local Conventions, if they thought proper to do so. He hoped they would, provided they were not too numerous; there is a danger of overdoing them, and he conceived that the advertising of a limited number of Conventions, to be held at stated intervals, would be the best means of preventing it; besides, such arrangements should, he thought, be made, as would prevent one Convention interfering with another. In the United States, they have their Annual State Conventions, but they arrange so that two do not occur at the same time. We have but one state, and it is proposed to have local Conventions all over; surely it will be well to make known or adopt a plan likely to prevent the occurrence of that circumstance here. In drawing up his resolutions, he had endeavoured to provide against a few of the difficulties and fears which had been experienced by the preliminary Committees in arranging for this Convention. From July last, when as Secretary of the sub-Committee of the Canada Sunday School Union he had issued his first circular relating to it, up to the moment of his arrival at Kingston, he had had to encounter many of these. He felt that each Committee should know from the beginning with whom to correspond, and upon whom to depend for co-operation. It would save a large amount of labour. Also, a few subjects should be suggested beforehand, so that parties may come prepared to discuss them. The selection of those named in the circular calling the present meeting, had caused a large amount of correspondence. Many topics were suggested. It had, therefore, been a delicate matter to make a selection, and impossible to make one to meet the wishes of all. There were other suggestions in the resolutions which he thought of value, and he was sorry that there appeared to be some misconception in relation to them. They did not *legislate* for future years as had been averred,—they simply recommended the holding of Conventions in certain years and certain places; the first in each place only being legislated for, and that only in the appointment of Committees to prepare for them. They to appoint Committees for those to succeed, and thus on time being anticipated, by one season only, and everything left open for the changes it effects. He would not, however, press his resolutions, but would be quite willing to agree to any motion which would be acceptable to the Convention.

On motion, the matter was referred to a Committee of Messrs. Taylor, Beadle, Logie, Nelson, Marling, and others with instructions to prepare a resolution on the subject.

FREE CONFERENCE.

The Convention then having disposed of the topics formally ordered to be discussed, entered upon a free conference.

A DELEGATE asked if it were proper to teach children their letters in Sunday Schools?

Mr. BEDWELL (Montreal) replied, by asking if children could read the gospel without learning how to read?

The DELEGATE who had asked the question thought the day too sacred to be employed on the alphabet, and considered that the time would be more fitly occupied in telling scriptural stories to the children.

A DELEGATE knowing that some children had no opportunity for instruction save in the Sunday School, would not think he did his duty if he did not teach children their letters.

A DELEGATE had heard many ways spoken of for getting children into the schools; but if he could learn how to get the aged in, he would go home contented.

Mr. B. LYMAN (Montreal) held that the only way by which the middle aged could be got into the schools, was by having the Spirit of God poured on them.

Rev. Mr. HODGSKIN (Doon) did not know that the best way to spend the Sabbath was to spend it publicly, and thought there was a danger of overlooking private and household piety. He sympathized with those who liked to see the Church filling the Sunday School; but no less with those who like to see Christians at home reading their Bibles. The best use of Sabbath Schools was in caring for uncared for children, and he did not wish to throw on them the whole

care that belonged to parents. He had two congregations—morning and afternoon, and the morning one had a school into which they collected all cared for or uncared for children. But the children of the other congregation were best instructed in the short catechism, because was done by their parents. While encourage the school then, let the household not be lost sight of.

Mr. HAGAR (Montreal) said he believed it would be found that those who attended most to the school, were also they who attended most to their household duties. He thought heads of families should be brought more than ever into the school, for children liked to see parents consistent and doing what they recommended. He remembered a school in the United States, where almost all the members of the Church attended. In one class there was no scholar under sixty years of age and they all wore spectacles.

Mr. BEGG (London,) recurring to the subject of rewards, said that if rewards were promised by God it was not for merit; but of grace. He would therefore, like to get rid of rewards of merit and have only gifts of affection.

A DELEGATE would like to use the word Sabbath always in the place of Sunday; taking the latter to be Heathenish and Popish and conveying a false idea.

Mr. TAYLOR on behalf of the Committee to which the ninth subject had been referred, presented the following resolution, which was carried.

" That this Convention cordially recommends the holding of general and local Conventions, and that the Hon. Jas, Ferrier, of Montreal, Mr. John Mair, M. D., of Kingston, Mr. Geo. Harcourt, of Toronto, and Mr. Wm. Begg, of London, be appointed a Committee, with full power to call a future Provincial Convention."

The CREDENTIAL COMMITTEE reported that they had examined the certificates of two hundred and sixty Delegates, all of which were duly filled up and certified, and had given certificates to three delegates whom they had good reason to regard as such from their respective schools. All these certificates had been countersigned by Benjamin Lyman, Esq., Secretary of the Committee, as required by the Railway authorities. The Committee did not attempt to classify the religious denominations.

On motion of Mr. MACALISTER, seconded by W. J. MORRIS.

It was ordered that a copy of the proceedings of the convention be sent to every school which responded to the circular of the preliminary committees by sending in statistics, but which have not been able to be represented in the Convention, and also to all other Sabbath Schools as far as possible.

On motion of Mr. TAYLOR, seconded by Dr. MAIR,—

It was resolved that James Stewart and Geo. Fenwick be appointed a Committee to obtain and audit the accounts of the hotel-keepers against delegates, so that they may be handed to the Mayor of the city of Kingston corrected if correction should be necessary.

On motion it was resolved, that while this Convention considers the Sabbath School to be a valuable aid to christian parents in the religious education of their children, yet it feels bound to express the opinion, that Sabbath School teachers cannot relieve parents from the divinely constituted obligation of attending to the religious education of their own children.

The BUSINESS COMMITTEE reported that they had referred to them letters from the Rev. E. Barrass, Primitive Methodist Minister at Toronto, and the superintendent of the first Baptist Church S. S. in that city, who were unable to be present, and recommended that the names of these and all others who had sent in similar communications should be entered on the minutes. The Committee had had several other communications and proposals before them, but as they referred to matters not strictly and appropriately coming within the province of the Convention, or which could not be taken up within the time, they have no report to present on them.

On motion, the thanks of the Convention were tendered to the Hon. James Ferrier for the eminent ability, courteousness and impartiality with which he had discharged the onerous duties of the Chair, and the Convention expressed the hope that he might be spared many years to continue his active labors in the cause of Sabbath Schools.

The Hon. JAMES FERRIER said that he had come there to perform a delightful duty, and had never felt so much honored as by the distinction conferred upon him. He hoped his soul had reaped benefit from Christian communion, and that he would go back a better man to the discharge of the duties of the School and of life.

The Chairman of the Business Committee the Rev. F. H. MARLING, then moved on their behalf :—

That the members of this Convention desire ere they separate from each other, to record the expression of their heartfelt thankfulness to Almighty God that his providence and grace have enabled them to assemble in such large numbers from every part of the Province, out of so many denominations of Christians, and to consult together with so much harmony and mutual benefit. "It has been good for us to be here," and we shall return to our homes and our schools, resolved in so far as in us lies, to bring the whole of the youth of Canada into these nurseries of the Church, with the hope that we may be instrumental in bringing them to Christ himself.

One affirmative feeling pervaded the Convention when this resolution was put.

After the singing of a hymn and prayer by the Rev. Mr. Chidlaw, who pronounced the benediction, the Convention dissolved.

———

A Meeting of the children of all the Sabbath Schools in Kingston, was held, in connection with the Convention, in the Wesleyan Methodist Church, at three o'clock. A good many delegates were present. The Rev. T. J. Hodgskin, Rev. Asa Bullard, Rev. B. W. Chidlaw, and Messrs. Thompson of Rochester, and Wilder of Detroit, addressed the children. The attention and singing of the latter were very pleasing. The meeting was one of great interest ; for it was felt, that the presence of Him, who delighteth to be with His people to bless them and to do them good, was not wanting.

... How many of the scho... are ...mbers of ... church?	11. How ... i...
...	Think a
...	Not any,
...	Several.
...	Cannot
...	Hard to
...	A small
...	Not kn
...	Few, if
...	About f
...	The ma
...	About t
...	Nearly
...	Not ma
...	About
...	Cannot
...	All cor
...	One-fo
...	Very f
...	Eight.
...	Say tv
...	Twelv
...	About
...	Forty
...	Many
...	Fifty.
...	None
...	Sever
...	None
...	Cant
...	Non
...een.	Tw
...	No
...	A r
...	Sev
...	No
...	Nii
...	Fif
...	On
...	No
...y-two ...	Ver
...	Thi
...	Noi
...een.	Eig
...	Thi
...	No
...	All
...	All
...	The
...ve.	Six
...	One
...y-four ...	Not
...	One
...	Six
...	A l
...	Not
...	Car
...	Son
...	Tw
...	Ten
...	Tw
...	Tw
...	Eig
...e.	One
...en.	Can
...	Not
...	One
...	
...	
...	Dor
...	No
...e.	Thi
...	Not
...	Dor
...	Not
...	Thi
...e.	Can
...	Not
...	Thi

SUMMARY OF THE PRECEDING SABBATH SCHOOL RETURNS.

1—Total number of Teachers.. 3203
2—Average attendance of Teachers.................................... 2652
3—Total number of Scholars.. 23349
4—Average attendance of Scholars.................................... 16669
5—Number of Scholars over 16 years of age........................... 2678
6—Number of Scholars under 6 years of age........................... 2333
7—Number of Schools which report an increase in the number of Scholars during the year.. 166

    Do   do   reported as being stationary.................... 68

    Do   do   which report a decrease in the number of Scholars during the year.. 25

    Do   do   reported as newly organized.................... 22

Increase of Scholars.. 2153
Number of scholars gathered into new Schools....................... 1497

                                                                3650
Decrease of scholars... 204

Total increase... 3446

    Of those who report favorably, but do not give figures, a few say "very large increase," a greater number say "large increase," the majority say "prosperous."

The decrease in some Schools is accounted for by the formation of new schools.

8—The number of Schools reported as closed during a portion of the year, is.... 39
Winter being the Season, and the time 2, 3, 4, 5 or 6 months.

9— Good many Schools report that they are suffering from particular causes, of these the following are observable :—

        Want of the Co-operation of parents.
        Want of Teachers.
        Want of Books.
        Sabbath School not appreciated.
        Priestly influence.

10—Number of Scholars reported as being members of the Church............. 1002

11—But few Schools return definite answers to the question "How many would not be under any religious instruction were it not for the Sabbath School." The character of the answers received, however, leads to the belief that the aggregate must be large. The answers in figures and per centages give 2900

12—Number of books in Libraries.................................... 67165

13—About 160 Schools reply that they have no Teachers' meetings. A majority of the balance report monthly meetings for prayer and business, a few report monthly meetings for each, several report weekly meetings for the study of the lesson and prayer and a good many report quarterly or irregular meetings.

14—The answers to the question "What is the average attendance of Teachers at the meeting," show that it is much higher at some Schools than it is at others. The general average is apparently below two-thirds.

15—Number of Conversions during the past year in the various Schools which have reported. 363

    A few scholars are alluded to as inquiring or under serious impression

16—123 Schools report that they are in the habit of doing something for missions.

    Several are supporting Orphans in India. The largest amount reported as collected in one School during the year, is £68 3s. 8d.

17—The answers to the question "Are the people in your vicinity alive to the importance of Sabbath Schools," are necessarily merely indicative. They show that much remains to be done for the Sabbath School cause in Canada.

DELEGATES PRESENT AT THE CONVENTION, KINGSTON.

February 11th, 12th and 13th, 1857.

The numbers before the names refer to the Statistical Returns.

```
 18—Ainsley, Richard ........ Wesleyan Methodist S. School.... Guelph.
226—Adams, Austin .......... Union S. School .............. Montreal.
191—Andrews,  G. W......... Wesleyan Methodist S. School ⎱
191—Anglin,  Wm........... Wesleyan Methodist S. School ⎰ Williamsville, near Kingston.
       Askew, Thos........... Church of England S. School... Kingston.
       Andrews, Joseph ....... Bible Christian S. School ..... Bowmanville.
       Amas, Andrew.......... Union S. School.............. Oshawa.
       Arksey, A............. Wesleyan  Methodist S. School.. Barrie.
150—Armstrong, E........... Wesleyan Methodist S. School.. Ottawa City.
267—Armstrong, II.......... Union  S. School ............ Edwardsburgh.
       Aylsworth, Robert ...... Union S. School ............. Odessa.
       Allice, A............. Bible  Christian S. School...... Oshawa.
    —Becket, J. C............ Canada S. School Union..... Montreal.
147—Burrell, John.......... Q. Sub. Wes. Meth. S. School... Montreal.
147—Bedwell, C. P......... Q. Sub. Wes. Meth. S. School.. Montreal.
148—Baylis, James.......... Congregational S. School ..... Montreal.
157—Boyd, J. T............ Free  Church S. School....... Brantford.
 92—Burpee, Revd. A......... Congregational S. School..... Montreal.
 71 ⎫
 72 ⎪
 73 ⎬ Beadle, Delos........... St. Catherine's S. School Union. St. Catherines.
 74 ⎭
  6—Bond, Hiram ............ Union S. School............. St. Vincent.
 19—Brebner, James......... Union S. School ............. Brooklyn.
 22—Best, Thomas.......... Union S. School............ ⎱
 22—Best William.......... Union S. School............ ⎰ Mount Pleasant Durham.
182—Byrne, James, junr ..... Congregational S. School..... Whitby.
186—Bartlett, Wm.......... Union S. School ........... North Ely.
183—Bone, Thomas F......... Wesleyan Methodist S. School.. Bowmanville.
       Begg, Wm ............. London S. School Union ..... London.
 20—Burns, Wm............. Free Church S. School....... Stratford.
111—Bird, James ......... Union S. School............ 1 Con. Co. of York, Playbro Cor's.
       Bellamy, J. B........... Union S. School............. North Augusta.
 49—Berry,  W. H.......... Baptist S. School ............ Hamilton.
       Bird, J.............. .............. Whitby.
       Barber, Chas.......... .............. Montreal.
227—Baker, John .......... Primitive Methodist S. School.. Bath.
222—Barnard, J............ Union S. School............. South Monaghan.
       Bredin  R ............. Wesleyan Methodist S. School.. Cobourgh.
       Benson,  J. R.......... Wesleyan Methodist S. School.. Peterboro.
       Bullard, Rev. A......... Massachusetts S. School Society. Boston.
252—Brooks, Wm........... Congregational S. School ..... Sherbrooke.
240—Betts, Rev. J. E........ Wesleyan Methodist S. School.. Quebec.
       Butler, John ........... Wesleyan Methodist S. School.. Brighton.
       Banthill, Moses .......... .............. Whitby.
       Barker, Rev. E........... .............. Eramosa.
       Beary, W. H............ .............. Hamilton.
       Bartlett, Wilder......... Union S. School............. Metcalfe Hill.
       Bround, John.......... .............. Brantford.
 14—Campbell,  Duncan ..... Union S. School............. Carleton Place.
 28—Cooper, Morris ......... Union S. School ............. Newcastle.
108—Craig, Wm............ Baptist S. School...... ....... Port Hope.
 90—Cade, Rev. M........... Primitive Methodist S. School.. Toronto.
147—Connelly, R........... Q. Sub. Wes. Meth. S. School... Montreal.
155—Christie, P............ Congregational S. School...... Green Island, W. Martintown.
156—Campbell, Robt......... Wesleyan Methodist S. School.. Brooklyn.
161—Croty, H............. Church of England S. School... Ingersoll.
166—Cleghorn, D........... Wesleyan Methodist S. School.. Port Hope.
178—Craig, R.............. Free Church S. School....... Cornwall.
194—Cash, D............. Congregational S. School..... Markham.
191—Clark, Jos............ Wesleyan Methodist S. School.. Kingston.
266—Caldwell, Thos......... London S. School Union........ London.
101—Campbell, P........... .............. Campbell's Corners.
       Chase, Jas............. Union S. School............. Oshawa.
       Chany, A............. Unknown................ Ogdensburgh, N. Y.
       Chown, S............. Wesleyan Methodist Central S.S. Kingston.
       Cosby, R............. Primitive Methodist S. School.. Kingston.
```

Cane, Robt.............United Presbyterian S. School..Yorkville.
Crony, John.............Free Church S. School.......Belleville.
Chidlaw, Rev. W. B.....American S. School Union....Cincinnatti, Ohio.
Comer, Jos.............Union S. School............Yonge St., Toronto.
56—Carman, Albert.........Wesleyan Methodist S. School..Matilda.
162—Clendinnen, Wm........G. Town Wes. Meth. S. School..Montreal.
Cochran, A.............Church of England S. School..Ingersoll.
246—Campbell, John.........Free Church S. School.......Montreal.
Chamberlain, Elias G....Wesleyan Methodist S. School..North Blenheim.
254—Cramley, John........:.United Presbyterian S. School..Belleville.
5—Calvin, —— ....Baptist S. School............Kingston.
36—Dorland, James.........Union S. School ....Percy.
43 }
44 } Dempsey, Rev. J........Baptist S. School............St. Andrews.
48—Davis, Paul.............Free Church S. School.......Hull.
142—Dersteen, John.........Union S. School.............South Wilmot.
187—Dickson, W.............Baptist S. School...........Montreal.
93—Dugdale, H.............Wesleyan Methodist S. School..Kingston.
191—Douglass, Rev. G........Wesleyan Methodist S. School..Kingston.
20—Dunn, Wm.............Free Church S. School.......Stratford.
102—Dayfoot, P. W..........Union S. School ....George Town
Dobson, P.............Baptist S. School............Port Hope.
105—Duncan, H.............Union S. School ....Camden.
Davis, J.............Union S. School ....Yonge St., Toronto.
248—Detler, G. H...........Wesleyan Methodist S. School..Napanee.
Dobbs, Rev. F. W.......Church of England S. School..Portsmouth.
Duggan, H.............   ....Kingston.
Douglas, Rev. J......Wesleyan Methodist S. School..Montreal.
154—Dobson, Peter..........   ....School Sec. No. 6, n.'r Hamilton
276—Demorest, D. L........   ....Harrington.
Denison, Rev. C. W.....Baptist S. School............Buffalo, N. Y.
40—Edwards, G...........Wesleyan Methodist S. School..Oshawa.
Elliot, Rev. J.............Canada S. Sch'l Union........Montreal.
138—Evans, H. J............Wesleyan Methodist S. School..Port Dover.
199—Edgan, W.............Congregational S. School.....Hamilton.
232—Edwards, James ....Wesleyan Methodist S. School..Barrie.
Evans, John..........   ....Toronto.
Ferrier, Hon. J..........Canada S. Sch'l Union........Montreal.
29—Fraser, Wm...........United Presbyterian S. School..Goderich.
39—Forrester, Jas..........Free Church S. School.......Melrose.
Fenwick, G. J..........Congregational S. School.....Kingston.
239—Fraser, Alex ....Union S. School.............Lancaster Front.
Fraser, Donald.........Union S. School.............Toronto.
Frost, John...........Wesleyan Methodist S. School..Owens Sound.
231—Ferguson, Willard.......Union S. School.............Duffin's Creek.
217—Ford, O.............Congregational S. School.....Newmarket.
Forster, Geo...........United Presbyterian S. School..Smith's Falls.
Fergusson, D..........Free Church S. School.......Montreal.
Fergusson, W..........   ....Kingston.
Foote, J. D............Massachusetts S. School Society..Buffalo, N. Y.
243—Foster, James.........Wesleyan Methodist S. School..Toronto.
218—Gibson, T. A...........Church of Scotland S. School..Montreal.
134—Goodfellow, P..........Free Church S. School.......Bradford.
45—Gelding, Geo..........Congregational S. School.....Toronto.
Grafton, F. G ....Congregational S. School.....Montreal.
63—Galway, S............St. L. Sub. Wes.Meth. S. Sch'l..Montreal.
Gordon, David..........   ....Pickering.
Grey, W.............Baptist S. School............Port Hope.
Gemmell, A...........Free Church S. School.......Toronto.
95—Goodhue, J. L..........Union S. School.............Danville.
Hagar, Geo...........Canada S. School Union........Montreal.
1—Hodgskin, Rev. T. J......Free Church S. School.......Doon.
42—Hibbard, P. V..........Union S. School.............St. Andrews
58—Hill, Thos.............Union S. School.............Lancaster.
106—Halloway ——..........Congregational S. School.....Brockville.
114—Hughes, G. S...........Union S. School.............Bowmanville.
119—Hinman, Smith.........Union S. School.............Cramahe.
200—Hyde, Levi J...........Union S. School.............Cramahe.
Hendrey, Thos..........Congregational S. School.....Mea'd. Road, Kingston.
Holmes, R. A...........Congregational S. School.....Kingston.
Hart, R. D.............Baptist S. School............Whitby.
145—Harcourt, Geo..........Congregational S. School.....Toronto.

Hamilton, Wm.........Church of Scotland S. School..Ottawa City.
Harpsee, Amos ....
Hurlburt, S..............   ....Perth.
Huntington, E. T........Unknown...............Rochester, N. Y.
Hill, R. N...............Union S. School...........North Gore.
Hone, Thos. S..........Wesleyan Methodist S. School..Bowmanville.
262—⎰   Union S. School............Kingsey.
264—⎱ Hethrington, J........Union S. School............Melbourne.
263—⎰   Union S. School............Durham.
Humphrey, Rev. J. L....   ....Malone, N. Y.
Herrick, Rev. J. R.......   ....Malone, N. Y.
24—Ives, J. M..........Union S. School.........Sec. No. 4, Cramahe.
131—Ironside, J. A..........   ....Fergus.
140—Irwin, R...............New Connection Me'dist S. Sch'l.Montreal.
146—Janes, D. P...........American Presbyterian S. S.....Montreal.
245—Jeffers, Rev. W........Wesleyan Methodist Central S.S.Montreal.
Jeffry, J.............Wesleyan Methodist Central S. S.Montreal.
Irwin, S. P...........Union S. School ....Aurora Co. York.
17—Kingston, Prof.........Wesleyan Methodist S. School..Cobourgh.
86—Kilpatrick, John ....Union S. School............Scarboro.
91⎱
89⎰ Kerr, Wm.............United Presbyterian S. School..Toronto.
178—Kilgour, J.............Free Church S. School.......Cornwall.
Keough, Rev. Thos.....Wesleyan Methodist S. School..Portsmouth, **near Kingston.**
Keith, Geo.............Free Church S. School.......Belleville.
Kay, Robt ....Aultsville.
Kilbourn, David ....Wesleyan Methodist S. School..Plattsville.
164—Louson, John ....Union S. School...........Montreal.
65—Lacy, W. P...........Primitive Methodist S. School ..Brampton.
171—Latimer, J. T...........Wesleyan Methodist S. School..North Gower.
146—Lyman, Benj.........American Pres. S. School......Montreal.
148—Lyman, S. Jones.......Congregational S. School......Montreal.
40—Lake, E. P............Wesleyan Methodist S. School..Oshawa.
47—Little, Cyrus...........Union S. School............Beamsville.
Luke, Jesse ....Oshawa.
Logie, Judge...........Church of Scotland S. School..Hamilton.
51—Lanton, Rev. H........Wesleyan Methodist S. School..Prescott.
Laughlin, A...........Wesleyan Methodist S. School..Toronto.
Lovelace, R...........Union S. School...........Scarboro.
Longman, Geo..........   ....Toronto.
Milloy, A.............Canada Sunday School Union..Montreal.
25—Minore, Wm ....Methodist Episcopal S. S.......Othro near Ottawa.
47—Merrill, M ....Union S. School............Beamsville.
67—Millard, Rev. Wm.......Plymouth Brethren S. S........Brampton.
88—Macalister, A...........Free Church S. School ....Kingston.
128—More, Wm...........Free Church S. School.......Quebec.
Miller, Rev. J. M........Unknown...............Ogdensburgh, N. Y.
·37—Mundell, A...........Free Church S. School ....Millbank.
189—Morgan, Wm..........Union S. School...........2d Con. Osnabruck.
201—Marling, Rev. F. H......Congregational S. School .....Toronto.
Massie, Wm...........Congregational S. School ......Montreal Village near Kingston.
35—Massey, W. A.........Wesleyan Methodist S. School..Newcastle.
Moore, Robt..........Union S. School............Emily.
11—Miller, Robt...........Wesleyan Methodist S. School..Montreal.
Murdock, Peter.........Free Church S. School.......Bowmanville.
273—Morris, W. J..........Church of Scotland S. School..Perth.
5—Mackie, Rev. J.........Baptist S. School............Kingston.
Mathewson, J. A.......Wesleyan Methodist S. School..Montreal.
Mortimer, Geo..........Congregational S. School......Newmarket.
Mackerras, Geo..........   ....Brockville.
228—Mattras, J.............Primitive Methodist S. School..Kingston.
Markham, Rev. J.......   ....Frontenac.
88—Mair, John, M. D........Free Church S. School........Kingston.
53—McLean, Hugh ....Union S. School ....Lancaster.
160—McDonald, Rev. G........Church of Scotland S. School..Fergus.
183—McCrae, John ....Wesleyan Methodist S. School..Bowmanville.
188—McKay, D.............United Presbyterian S. School..Montreal.
McPhail, Ed...........New Connection Me'd'st S. Sch'l.Toronto.
McKillican, Rev. J.......Congregational S. School......Martintown.
McNairn, J. N..........Wesleyan Methodist S. School..Dickinson's Landing.
McFarlane, D...........Free Church S. School.......Dundas.
McKechnie, R...........Free Church S. School........St. Andrews.

McNevin, John..........Union S. School..............Emily.
McFarlane, C.............. ....Melrose.
260—McDonald, W. K.........Union S. School............Edwardsburgh.
McPhaul, —— ....Free Church S. School.......Kingston.
Norman, Hugh ....Union S. School..............Loydtown.
70—Nasmyth, Wm..........Baptist S. School..........Woodstock.
146—Nelson, H. A.............American Pres. S. School......Montreal.
209—Naylor, Frances ....Baptist S. School..............Trafalgar Settlement.
265—Neilson, Geo.............. ....Belleville.
136—Oliver, W. H.............Wesleyan Methodist S. School..Paris.
O'Laughlin, A. J............Church of England S. School..Kingston.
Oliver, Geo. H..........Church of England S. School..Kingston.
Oliver, Andrew..........Wesleyan Methodist S. School..North Blenheim.
117—Pardee, A. P............Union S. School..............North Augusta.
141—Pritcherd, Rev. S. W....Baptist S. School ....Font Hill.
147—Pickup, E..............Q. Sub. Wes. Meth. S. School...Montreal.
Parslow, John ....St. L. Sub. Wes. Meth. S. Sch'l..Montreal.
180—Pearson, W. H..........Wesleyan Methodist S. School..Toronto.
188—Paton, Laird............United Presbyterian S. School..Montreal.
220—Price, R. B.............Union S. School .... Bath.
Pearson, P. P...........Union S. School ....Newmarket.
Purkiss, Geo............Union S. School ....Dickinson's Landing.
Plumerfield, Geo........Wesleyan Methodist S. School..Markham.
211—Paterson, D.............United Presbyterian S. School..Beverly.
Parker, J...............Union S. School............Camden.
Pomroy, Dan............Methodist Episcopal S. School..Kingston.
Pearson, F. T............. ....Toronto.
251—Paton, John............Church of Scotland S. School ..Kingston.
9—Pomroy, R. D............Methodist Episcopal ....Brockville.
78—Popham, Wm............Union S. School............Osgoode, Metcalfe Co.
209—Purdy, Hiram ....Union S. School ....Cramahe.
Porte, W. J............. ....Picton.
Patton, J. junr...........Wesleyan Methodist S. School..Toronto.
41—Roblin, Rev. P. J........Union S. School............Shannonville.
87—Roberts, E.............Bible Christian S. School ......Cobourg.
106—Robinson, Rev. R........Congregational S. School......Brockville.
120—Rogerson, John..........Congregational S. School......Bowmanville.
Randall, Peter..........Baptist S. School..........Port Hope.
Rutherford, Robinson ....Wesleyan Methodist S. School..Peterboro.
204—Rose, Daniel............Wesleyan Methodist S. School..Morrisburg.
Scott, S. B.............Canada S. S. Union..........Montreal.
46—Sim, Rev. A.............Congregational S. School......St. Andrews.
79—Sackville, Wm..........Union S. School ....Bloomfield, South Monaghan.
86—Stevenson, John ....Union S. School..............Scarboro.
106—Shepherd, —— ....Congregational S. School......Brockville.
122—Squelch, J. W..........Union S. School ....Brock.
58—Stewart, James..........Free Church S. School ....Kingston.
55—Steed, Robt..............Union S. School............Sarnia.
191—Schroder, J..............Wesleyan Methodist S. School..Kingston.
191—Savage, J..............Wesleyan Methodist S. School..Kingston.
191—Stewart, Geo...........Wesleyan Methodist S. School..Kingston.
Scott, Rev. John........Union S. School ....Bath.
Smith, Sidney N........Wesleyan Methodist S. School..Odeltown.
64—Stewart, P. A..........Baptist S. School............Breadalbane.
Shortt, Rev. Jonathan....Church of England S. School..Port Hope.
30—Stevenson, H. Jas........Primitive Methodist S. School..Toronto.
Snell, Elias ....Union S. School............Chincouche.
Singleton, A. C..........Wesleyan Methodist S. School..Brighton.
Shaw, W. W.............. ....
Sleith, Robt.............Wesleyan Methodist S. School..Sarnia.
237—Sherwood, Sheriff........Free Church S. School ....Brockville.
Scott, Jos.............Union S. School ....Bath.
177—Shepherd, Wm. junr......Methodist Epis. S. School......Hamilton.
Smart, Rev. Wm........Union S. School ....Gananoque.
Sexsmith, John O........Union S. School ....Richmond, E. T.
Sutton, S. P............Baptist S. School ....Brantford.
Sills, Rev. W. A......... ....Brockville.
Savage, H. G............. ....Williamsville.
Taylor, Jas. W..........Canada S. S. Union............Montreal.

84--Truesdell, J. W. {
........Union S. School ....Little Warwick.
........Union S. School ....Big Warwick.
........Union S. School ....5th Range Durham.
........Union S. School ....Hardwood Hill.
........Union S. School ....Goshen, Windsor.
}

127—Treadwell, Sheriff.........Union S. School ....L'Original.
80—Turnbull, James.........Union S. School ....S. Monaghan.
Turnbull, J.........Union S. School ....Sec. No. 4, do.
230—Torrance, Rev. R.......United Presbyterian S. School..Guelph.
Thomson, Rev. J.........Wesleyan Methodist S. School..Bradford.
112—Thomas, H.............Primitive Methodist S. School..Clairville.
Thomson, J. H............Unknown ....Roc'ester, N. Y.
121—Van Vlick, T.............   ... .Lacolle.
85—Wallace, A..............Baptist S. School ....Highland Creek, Scarboro
94—Wood, Rev. J...........Congregational S. School .....Brantford.
100—Witze, Jos.............Union S. School ....Yonge and Escot.
104—Wallis, J. W...........Congregational S. School......Humber.
104—Ward, S. R............Congregational S. School......Humber.
129—Weyner, Jas............Wesleyan Methodist S. School..Brantford.
139—Walker, John...........New Connection Me'd'st S. Sch'l..Montreal.
144—Walker, James ....Free Church S. School ....Hamilton.
163—Wilson, Sam ....G. Town Wes. Meth. S. School.Montreal.
166—Whitney, Rev. R.......Wesleyan Methodist S. School..Port Hope.
187—Williams, Rev. J. N.....Baptist S. School ....Montreal.
197—Woolley, Robt..........Methodist Epis. S. School......Matilda.
201—Wey, Jos. W...........Congregational S. School......Toronto.
Windatt, Wm............Bible Christian S. School .....Bowmanville.
Wales, H. R.............Congregational S. School .....Markham.
4—Whitley, Wilson........Baptist S. School ....Whitby.
White, Jas.............   ....Whitby.
201—Woodhouse, J. Joseph....Congregational S. School......Toronto.
Wilson, Rev. D.........Baptist S. School ....Farmersville.
White, Ed.............Union S. School............Grimsby.
Wallis, Jos.............Church of Scotland S. School ..Etobicoke.
221—Wood, J..............Wesleyan Methodist S. School..Wolf Island.
51 }
52 } Warden, Wm ....United Schools..............Salem.
15—Wilson, Rev. A.........Church of Scotland S. School..Kingston.
Wilson, R..............Union S. School ....Thomasburgh.
Wilder, E. C............Unknown ....Detroit, Michigan.

RECAPITULATION.

Representing Union Sabbath Schools.....	76	Representing Amer. Pres. Church S. Sch'ls.	3
" Wesleyan Methodist S. Sch'ls	64	" Methodist Epis. S. Schools...	5
" Church of England S. Sch'ls.	7	" Sabbath Schools in the U. S.	5
" Congregational Church S. S.	30	" Plymouth Brethren S. Sch'l .	1
" Free Church S. Schools.....	25	" Sabbath Sch'l Organizations.	14
" Baptist Sabbath Schools	19	" Schools—the denominational	
" Primitive Methodist S. Sch'ls.	7	characters of which are un-	
" United Presbyterian Ch. S. S.	8	known to the compiler....	30
" Church of Scotland S. Sch'ls.	8		
" New Con. Methodist S. S....	3		310
" Bible Christian S. Schools...	5		

STATISTICS or Communications were received from the following. The majority intimated the probability of their own attendance or the attendance of others, many stated that they were delegated.

The numbers before the names refer to the Statistical returns.

21—Armstrong, John,........Union S. School..............Eramosa.
175—Anderson, Alex..........Not known ....Percy.
412—Allan, J................Free Church S. School ....Perth.

158—Adams, James .... Not known .... Embro.
108—Bardall, P .... Baptist S. School .... Port Hope.
33—Blackader, John .... Union S. School .... Windsor.
    Black, James .... Not known .... Beverly.
165—Brown, Thomas .... Wesleyan Methodist S. School. . Toronto.
195—Bingham, Alfred .... Wesleyan Methodist S. School. . Waterdown.
    Best, — .... Not known .... London.
208—Brown, George .... Not known .... Milton.
210—Bain, Rev. J .... Church of Scotland S. School . . Scarboro.
215—Brown, James .... Not known .... Odeltown.
224—Barnes, C. J .... Wesleyan Methodist S. School. . Markham.
8—Brown, P. D .... Amer. Presbyterian Branch S.S. . Montreal.
10—Beach, Lyman .... Not known .... North Dundee.
61—Bothwell, T. .... Not known ....
77—Beattie, J. M .... Baptist S. School .... Toronto.
96—Boomer, Alfred .... Wesleyan Methodist S. School. . Wellesly Hawkesville.
97—Bartlett, Russel .... Union S. School .... Smith's Falls.
172—Bridgman, J. W .... Science Hill.
179—Barker, Jas .... Free Church S. School .... Ingersoll.
6—Cunningham, Stephen .... Union S. School .... St. Vincent.
130—Chamberlin, — .... Not known .... Wilmot.
68—Can, Wm .... Not known .... Canton Hope.
169—Camp, D. W .... Not known .... Smithville, Lincoln.
185—Clumpet, Richardson .... Union S. School .... South Durham.
81—Dexter, A. .... Union S. School .... Cavan.
152—Duncan, David .... Not known .... Egmondsville.
225—Davis, Jas .... Methodist Episcopal S. School. . Willow Dale.
109—Dickinson, W. D .... Congregational S. School ...... Prescott.
25—Faulkner, Joseph .... New Con. Methodist S. School. . Hamilton.
22—Fullerton, S. .... Union S. School .... Toronto.
233—George, James .... Wesleyan Methodist S. School. . Bradford.
54—Graham, John .... 2 Con. Ormstown.
83—Goodwillie, D. H .... Union S. School .... Stamford.
153—Gould, Carman M .... Carleton.
195—Griffin, G. D .... Wesleyan Methodist S. School. . Waterdown.
268—Hodgson, Jas .... Not known .... Whitby.
26—Hutton, Jno .... Wesleyan Methodist S. School. . Vienna.
53—Haight, C. .... Not known .... Peden.
115—Henry, Albert .... Oshawa.
168—Hamilton, John .... Church of Scotland S. School . . Beachville.
126—Hartman, John, M. P. P. . . New Con. Methodist S. School. . Aurora, County of York.
126—Irwin, — .... New Con. Methodist S. School. . Aurora, County of York.
2—Johnson, E. R. .... Episcopal Methodist S. School. . Farmersville.
13—Johnston, W. A. .... Union S. School .... Toronto.
99—Kennedy, G. H .... Charleston, Hatley.
281—Kanie, John .... Dungannon.
83—Lutz, Morris C .... Free Church S. School .... Galt.
170—Lenfestey, P. .... Wesleyan Methodist S. School. . Owens Sound.
60—Lonsdale, Rev. A .... Episcopal S. School .... Laprairie.
205—Meysay, D .... Brampton, Gore.
223—Murphy, J .... Episcopal Methodist S. Shool. . Farmersville.
229—Morn, D .... 3 Con. Kingston Township.
334—Mickle, John .... Union S. School .... Woolwich.
344—Morris, Alex .... Church of Scotland S. School . . Montreal.
3—Mitchell, G .... Farmersville.
34—Maginn, Charles .... Union S. School .... Toronto.
113—Millie, Edward .... Union S. School .... Sec. 6 Township of Arran, C. W.
149—Manny, Wm .... Wesleyan Methodist S. School. . Montreal.
181—Mason, W. J. .... Wesleyan Methodist S. School. . Peterboro.
118—Moullin, J. B. .... Union S. School .... Coaticook.
192—Martin, Leonard .... Not known .... Coaticook.
16—Mackie, Thomas .... Not known .... Leeds.
14—McLaren, Peter .... Union S. School .... Carletonplace.
45—McIlbean, John .... Not known .... Martintown.
214—McDonald, John .... Church of Scotland S. School. . Oakville.
38—McDougall, G. .... Free Church S. School .... Bowmanville.
167—McGregor, J. .... Free Church S. School .... Port Dover.
174—McLaughlan, Arch. ...... Not known .... Southwold, by Fingall.
176—McKay, Thos. .... Union S. School .... New Edinburgh.
202—McGregor, M .... Union S. School .... Athol, Glengarry.
    McCormick, R. C .... New York.

203—Noble, B...................Not known..................Haldimand.
219—Phillips, Robert..........United Presbyterian S. School..Napanee.
193—Porteous, M..............Union S. School.............St. Louis DeGonzaque.
100—Parish ——...............Union S. School.............Yonge & Escot.
      Playfair, Jno...........Not known..................Bathurst.
196—Parish, Agra.............Union S. School.............Farmersville.
341—Rowland, J...............Wesleyan Methodist S. School..Toronto.
342—Rowell, George...........Wesleyan Methodist S. School..Yorkville.
66—Robinson, W. S............Bible Christian S. School.....Whitby.
103—Robson, John.............................Bayfield.
137—Robertson, J.............................Perth.
89—Reed, Dr..................Not known..................Thornhill.
335—Stovel, Wm. ....Baptist S. School...........Guelph.
27—Stephens, Sylvanus........Union S. School.............Vienna.
33—Sanderson, Rev. R.........Episcopal Methodist S. School..Othro.
50—Simpson, Thomas...........Not known..................Township of Lambton.
139—Sargison, G..............Not known..................Montreal.
      Sheffield, Thos..........Not known..................Beverly.
212—Thome, D.................Bible Christian S. School.....Orono.
247—Wooton, John.............Baptist S. School...........Simcoe.
69—Walker, D.................Church of Scotland S. School..Sarnia.
132—Wilson, Thos.............Union S. School.............Troutbrook, Ringwick.
151—White, Rev. C............Wesleyan Methodist S. School..Smithville.
159—Waddell, Geo.............Not known..................Plympton.
136—Young, Thomas G..........Not known..................Pittsburgh.
107—Yeomans, D. P............Union S. School.............Millcreek, Odessa.

The following, the majority of whom sent in statistics, expressed great interest in the Convention and their regrets that they would not be able to attend :—

207—Rev. R. L. Tucker........Wesleyan Methodist S. School..Strathroy.
269—William Stevens..........Not known..................Smithtown, Peterboro.
278—John McWaters............Congregational S. School.....Stratford.
277—Thomas Elliott...........Union S. School.............No. 6 S. Sec., Forrister's Falls.
31—John Paton................Union S. School.............Malden, Essex Co. Amherstburgh.
116—Andrew Wooler............Union S. School.............Windsor Mills.
125—H. E. Cromer.............Union S. School.............Melbourne Ridge.
1—R. Ferrie, M. P. P.........Free Church S. School.......Doon.
206—Jos. T. Wenbrock.........Union S. School.............Bolton.
62—S. A. Hurd................Congregational S. School.....Eaton, C. E.
184—R. Kneeshaw..............Wesleyan Methodist S. School..Ingersoll.
59—John McLeod...............Not known..................Shipton, Scotch Settlement.
275—John Clark...............Free Church S. School.......Dundas.
76—Isaac Piper...............Not known..................Salford.
7—Samuel Orr................Union S. School.............Lachute.
12—Rev. Wm. King.............Free Church S. School.......Buxton.
75—J. Bowes..................Union S. School.............Ingersoll.
143—Wm. Millar...............Not known..................Farrall's Corners.
261—J. Hall..................Free Church S. School.......Peterboro.
133—Wm. M. Christie..........Union S. School.............Chippewa.
271—J. Somerville............Wesleyan Methodist S. School..Huntingdon.
272—Andrew Stevenson.........Wesleyan Methodist S. School..Ferguson's Falls, Lanark.
      George Braud...........Primitive Methodist S. School..Guelph.
      Ira Vancamp............Not known..................Bowmanville.
      Wm. W. Anderson........Not known..................N. Gwilliambury.
      H. Seymour.............Not known..................Renfrew.
      Rev. G. Colwell........................Tweed.
      Rev. J. Byrne..........Congregational S. School.....Whitby.
      V. A. Coleman..........Not known..................Castleton.
      Wm. Anderson...........Not known..................5th Con. Lochiel.
      John W. Higginson......Not known..................Hawkesbury.
      Rev. W. Gregg..........Free Church S. School.......Belleville.
98—Josiah Purkiss...........Not known..................Thornhill.
      Rev. E. Barrass........Primitive Methodist S. School..Toronto.